I would like to dedicate this book to our police officers. You all are, and always will be, the shield of our society. Without all that you do, all that you suffer through, and all your families do, our country would truly be lost. Please know that you are appreciated and supported. Be strong and Goddess bless you all.

Also, to my wonderful grandparents, who supported my dreams both financially and emotionally, I love you both.

I would also like to formally acknowledge and thank the following people who gave me their permission to use their likenesses to form my characters. Without you all, they wouldn't exist: Michael Hockings, Jeffrey Bulian, J.L. Wolf, and D. Fromherz, thank you all from the bottom of my heart.

Prologue

Joshua and Morgan laughed and shoved each other, wandering through the trails in the forested hills of Crystal Cove State Park. Joshua, the younger of the two, had just learned how to hike and how to survive outside, thanks to his older brother's knowledge. The trees rustled and creaked as the wind danced through the branches of the forest. As close together as the trees stood, it found no difficulty swirling around their thick trunks. The breeze whistled and howled as it blew, trying to squeeze through the gaps in the trees. The moon light cast shadows through the foliage of the trees canopy, leaving little patches of shimmering light on the path. As the wind blew, the patches seemed to dance their own little dance on the ground beneath the brothers' feet.

The moonlight struck a small gem, buried down in the dirt that had been trampled by the animals that walked the trail. The glimmer of metal caught Joshua's eye as they walked. Kneeling down, he dusted off the area around the small object. When he had freed it from the soil, he scooped it into his hand, and turned to face his brother, who had kept walking. He jogged to catch up and presented the necklace, saying "Morgan, check this out?"

Curious at his little brother's find, Morgan turned to face him. Seeing the glimmering necklace, he held out his hand and motioned for it. When Josh gave it to him, Morgan looked at it, squinting his eyes and trying to make out every detail. He turned to the moon and held it against the light, making it easier to see. It was a necklace with a jeweled charm as the only adornment. The chain itself was not a chain, but several pieces of black leather, woven together around each other to form a solid rope. In the center of it sat a silver charm, roughly the diameter of a golf ball. The silver was laced with slender golden veins. In the center of the silver sat a large, blood red stone.

"Looks nice, bro. Hold onto it until tomorrow, then we can see if anybody's missing it. If not, it'll make a good gift for mom. " He handed the necklace back to Josh, who put it in the pocket of his wind breaker jacket. He looked back to his brother, who had turned away, looking at the forest around him. He stiffed his back and he looked back at Josh, saying

"Let's get moving. The wind's picking up and it's getting colder."

As they kept down the trail toward the beach, the wind took a violent turn. It began whipping and whistling as if a storm was blowing in off the cove. Branches began waving in the wind, and some began to snap off. The once playful specks of light danced with frenzy as the wind beat the leaves with savagery. Suddenly, a chilling laugh caused them to stop dead in their tracks. The boys turned their heads behind them as another wave of laughter arose from the darkness behind them, carried by the wind to where they stood. Morgan took unsheathed his hunting knife from where it lay hidden under his jacket. Scanning the forest, he gripped the handle harder and shouted out into the woods, "Who's out there?!"

Hearing nothing, he licked his lips and whispered to Joshua "You still got that necklace?"

A tiny voice whispered back "Yeah, why?"

"Let me see it real quick." Holding out his hand toward his brother, he kept his eyes on the tree lines around them.

Handing his big brother the necklace, Joshua became increasingly frightened at their surroundings. The animals went quiet, yet all around them branches were snapping and the brush was rustling. The darkness began to hang heavy on them, chilling their bones. Looking up, Josh became increasingly alarmed to see that a dark, heavy cloud had rolled over the moon, blocking the light. He looked back to Morgan, who had just severed the cord of the necklace, and slipped the gem into his upturned hand. His face lit up with the small flame of his lighter as he fused the cord back together,

Josh silently wondered what was going on in his brother's head.

Morgan looked at his little brother and handed the gem back to him. He whispered, "Whatever happens, keep this safe."

Joshua nodded and opened his mouth to speak, but a twitch of movement caught his eye. He gazed past his brother as a twisted, white shape emerged from the woods.

The creature stood on two legs, long and gangly, yet wired with muscle. Its torso was long and twisted, as if the body had been mangled in some way. The arms hung down by its sides, long and gangly, yet bulging with muscles. The monsters fingers were slender, and the nails came to fine black points that gleamed with a wicked sharpness.

The worse feature was the face: Long and stark white, with ears that rose to points that almost resembled horns. Coming out from either temple, were two twisted black horns that sprung from his head. Two black disks sunk into the sickly white face. The pupils sparkled a brilliant red. When the creature smiled, it revealed a row of twisted, sharp, black teeth. Bile rose in Josh's throat as he stared motionless, locked in place by a feeling of raw fear as he gazed upon the monster.

However, it wasn't long before he snapped out of the trance and screamed a blood curdling scream. He pointed to the trees behind Morgan, who had already whipped around to face the being. One gangly arm raised up and pointed at the two as another grizzly, twisted laugh fell from its mouth.

Morgan's face paled as he shouted "Run! Head to the beach, GO!"

The wind tore through the trees as they raced down the dirt trails that wove through the hills of Crystal Cove State park. Joshua looked behind them as they cut right, racing down a wooded trail. Josh could hear Morgan cursing loudly as they ran, and he didn't blame him. The trees were so closely packed together that the branches smacked into their faces and drew blood. One had managed to cut Josh's eyebrow, causing blood to run down into his eye, stinging his eyes and blurring his vision.

Jumping over a fallen log, he risked a look behind them. His eyes widened as he spotted the creature jumping and dodging the trees. He doubled his speed, against his body's protest. His lungs began to hurt with each breath that he drew. The longer he ran, his speed began to fail and his legs threated to give out from under him. A feeling of dread came over him as he watched Morgan jump over the small creek bed. He gathered all the remaining strength he could muster. He jumped just fine, but when he had to land, his legs finally gave out. He rolled into the clearing, stopping face down in the grass. He looked up and cried out "Morgan!"

Morgan stopped, and whipped his head around, his own chest rising and falling because of his heavy breathing. He looked at his little brother, and raced back to the small clearing. He knelt down and helped his brother to his feet, the placed his hands on his shoulders. He looked at Josh and said "Run bro, get the hell out of here." A small, breathless Josh replied "WH-What about you Morgan?"

"I'm going to buy you some time."

With that, he turned around and shouted at the mysterious creature, who stood just after the small creek bed. "Come on, I'm not scared of you,

you stupid fuck! You want a fight, well now you've got one!" He redrew his knife and stood in the clearing, with his back to Josh, who turned around and bolted down the trail, tears streaming down his face.

When he was a decent distance away, Joshua heard the laughter, and looked back, ducking down behind some old oak trees that had collapsed and now lay against each other, forming a niche that Josh could look through without being on the direct trail. Morgan stood bathed in moonlight, knife in hand. Just past his shoulder stood that pale, twisted creature, half hidden from sight in the dark shadows. His brother rolled the knife through his hand a couple times, then he stepped forward and took up a weak guard. In response, the creature with a smooth, almost practiced motion, closed the gap between them with one effortless stride and swatted the weapon out of his grip. Josh looked in terror as he saw the gleam of joy in that creature's large, shiny eye. With lightning fast speed, he wrapped one hand wrapped around Morgan's neck. Effortlessly, Morgan was lifted off the ground by his throat and thrown toward Joshua.

Seeing his brother land on his back, unable to move or breathe, Joshua turned and ran. Behind him the twisted, cackling laughter of the demon rang on the wind, followed by the blood curdling screams and the sound of flesh being ripped and torn apart. Josh pumped his arms and ran as far as he could step, tears wetting his face and blurring his vision. He shoved branches and tree limbs from his face as they slapped and scratched against his skin.

Finally breaking onto the beach, Josh let out a horrified scream, attracting the attention of a small group of people having a bonfire. He collapsed from exhaustion, causing a commotion as the people approached. As he lay in the sand, the charm that hung on the necklace originally slide out of his pocket and laid itself to rest in the sand, covered by the sand kicked up as the people surrounded him.

As the crowd grew in size, the creature broke off his pursuit and watched from the shadowed trees. The last thing Josh heard as he fell into unconsciousness was a whispered rhyme "Things are in motion, you cannot deny. Soon the Freak will take and break down the sky." Laughter drifted away in the wind.

Chapter One: A Bad Shadow.

"Hey Jack, Heads up!" A volleyball flew toward the strawberry blonde head of Jackson Williams. A 6'2 beanstalk, Jackson ducked the ball and dove, knocking it back into the air. Laughing, he shot back "Nice try big guy, but I'm quicker than that!" Returning fire was the near 7 foot tall giant, Mikey Sterling. The two played a one v. one sand volleyball game. Their fast and furious motions kicked up clouds of golden sand and waves of laughter. As the ball sailed back to Mike, Jack mumbled a quick spell and had the sunlight reflect off the ball's gleaming white surface. Mike grunted as the light hit him, but he managed to bump the ball back into the air and break the line. He leapt forward and went to strike it back. Jack dodged out of the way as the ball dove toward a small sand dune. A wave of sand shot into the air as Mike laughed and said "30 all. My dear brother, it seems you're getting slower by the point."

Jack picked it up and replied "At least I'm still quicker than you big guy."

Their boisterous laughter carried on the wind towards two women sunbathing by the water. They laid out on two beach loungers under one large umbrella. The taller one was deep in her reading, and the shorter of the two was drawing on a pad of paper. The shorter of the two set her pad down, looked over the top rim of her sunglasses and said "Serenity, do you think we should intervene before our men kill each other?

Serenity sighed, closed her finger on her page, and replied "I'm on vacation Jas, so nah. They can be big boys and manage their power."

The two chuckled and sunk back into silence. Jas looked down at her newest piece: A lacey wrap that she tattooed around her thigh. The freshly healed reds and whites shown brilliantly in the sun. Serenity reopened her book and resumed reading, enjoying the moment of peace. After a few moments, she commented "This breeze is wonderful. It so soft and gentle."

Jas nodded her agreement and added "We've got a good day for this overall. The sun is shining nice and bright, the sea waters are crystal clear, and the sand is nice and warm." She sighed "Today is a good day." She snuggled down deeper into her lounger and looked back down at her sketch pad, tapping the pencil to the paper.

Further on down the beach, a stocky man approached the camp, carrying several big bags full of food. When he got close enough, he let loose a piercing whistle, catching their attention. Jack saw the man coming, he called out, "Hey Serenity, Jas; the food's here." The two women looked towards them, and seeing the boy coming back with food, they got up and walked over to the rustic picnic table in the center of their site. The sun caught on the Jas's fiery red hair as she hollered "Mikey, don't hit so hard, you'll take his head off."

Mike looked at her and said "If you wanna see me take his head off Jas baby, just ask." Turning back to Jack, Mike dug in and jumped, spiking the ball with as much force as he could muster. Ducking the heat-packed spike, Jack rolled under the net and ran towards an old, rustic looking picnic table. Feeling his stomach rumble and churn, he sat down. As the food carrier got closer, he called out "Hey Jeff, what'd ya bring us?!"

Jeff shot back "Back off Jack, this is all my shit. You shoulda brought your own!"

"I gave your ass the money for this stuff, fork my shit over ya dick."

Suddenly, Serenity walked over and chimed in "Boys, boys please, we are all hungry." When she was close enough to them, she snatched the bags out of Jeff's hands and stuck her tongue out, saying "Now you two can fight, because our lunch is safe." Jack smiled at her, then tackled Jeff. They rolled around and grappled in the sand for a few moments, trying to use different holds to make the other submit. Jack had just locked Jeff in a headlock, when two giant, forceful hands broke the hold and separated them apart. A deep chuckle rolled from Mike's throat as he said "Guys, it's a vacation. Let's stop fighting for once and eat eh?"

Jas got up from her seat and around the table to them. She said "Yeah, the big guy is right. Settle down or I'm shoving my umbrella up both your asses." Jack chuckled and said "Fine, fine. I'll keep him alive for a while longer."

Jeff laughed and nodded his head, saying "I was gonna say the same thing to you." Mike nodded in satisfaction. They shook hands, and then Mike released their shoulders in favor of his sandwich, which Jas was holding out for him to take. Licking their lips, they joined hands in a circle and Jack said "We give thanks to our goddess for the sunlight that graces our faces, The soft water that licks our feet, and this great meal we are about to receive." With the grace said, they all unwrapped their sandwiches and tore into them with great intensity. Bread crumbs and chip pieces flew everywhere as they ate and the only sound to be heard was the rustle of wrapping paper and chip bags, with the occasional hiss of a pop tab being opened. In short order, the assorted foot long sandwiches were reduced to crumbs on paper and stains on napkins; and once full soda cans were crumpled and smashed, then tossed to the center of the table, where Mike had built a pyramid with the metal. Finally coming up from his finished food, Jack sighed and let loose a long winded belch, flowed by a sigh of contentment and happiness.

One by one, the others finished their food and sat up, away from the pile of sandwich wrappers. Jas let loose a loud belch and flexed her arm, showing off her new Celtic cross tattoo that wrapped around her bicep as she said "I'm manlier than any of you." Mikey looked at his girlfriend and laughed, shaking his head. He asked "If you're a man, then what does that make me?"

"My bitch, baby." Jas stuck her tongue out at him and then laughed.

Jeff looked around the table to all present and said "Hey, isn't anyone going to thank me for bringing you all this glorious meal?"

Serenity snorted "Don't get a big head, Blonde Boy, me and Jack gave you the money." She scooted closer to her long time mate and secret future husband. He smiled down at her and chided, "Darling, it's alright." He turned toward Jeff and joked, "Hey, thanks for driving to subway and remembering so many orders."

"Yeah well at least I can drive a stick shift." Jeff flexed his hand in response and grinned smugly at Jack.

"I can stop that real quick." Jack's eyes flashed as the palm of his hand began to glow softly, surging with magic. His mind began working to prepare a hex to place on Jeff's driving, when Jas sighed and said, "Will you boys put your dicks away please? This pissing contest is over." Serenity piped up, "Hey, Jacks dick is mine. No one else can see it." She blushed red as she realized what she said. Mike hooted with laughter and said "Well, little sister isn't as innocent as she seems!" They all started busting out laughing as Serenity's face grew bright red and she buried her face into Jack's shoulder Mike and Jeff's fists pounded on the table as they attempted to catch their breath through their laughter. Jasmine had tears in her eyes as her face glowed red. Even Jack chuckled a bit before he wrapped his arm around her and sighed, saying "It's alright dear, they're just jealous."

Mike was gasping for air when he said "What? We're jealous of a little string bean, that's rich." His laughter increased and he rocked back, holding his sides. Suddenly, his arms started failing as he rocked back too far and fell from his seat laughing, which caused the rest of group to start laughing even harder.

When the laughter finally subsided, Mike picked himself up out of the sand and sighed, wiping away a tear from his eye. As he was dusting off the sand from his back, he sat back down between his brother and Jas and said "This is what we needed: Good food, Family, Fun under the sun and no demons or scary monsters to beat down and banish. Finally, some fucking time off." Jas snickered at the slight Scottish accent that he took as he swore. Jeff shook his head and raised his can of soda "I'll drink to that laddie." He mocked his brother's Scottish tone and smiled. Serenity raised her face from Jack's shoulder and raised her can, still red from embarrassment, she added "To our family, a complete bunch of assholes."

Jack raised his can and said "To this world, may it ever stand."

Jas raised her can and said "To our wolves, it's good to be one."

The family smiled and cried out, "Here, Here!" before drinking deeply.

When the toast ended, Jack got up from the table and walked over to where he parked his black, four door pick-up and started it up. Putting it in reverse, he backed it up close to the table. Once it was back to the group, he put the battery on and opened all the doors. He flipped through the radio until he found a local classic rock station. Cranking the speakers up to full, he got out and jumped into the bed. He took up an air guitar as he danced to some old Bon Jovi in the truck bed. His antics were only fueled when Mike jumped up with him and danced with him. Serenity looked at the two of them and shook her head. Sighing, she looked to Jasmine and asked "Do you ever just sit back and think 'Wow, I chose that man?'"

 Jas nodded and half sighed, half laughed as she replied "All the time."

She looked at her current lover, Mike, who was dancing along to an old ACDC song with a big, goofy grin plastered all over his face. She walked over and got dragged into dancing with him. Soon, the entire group was making music with their combined laughter.

Suddenly, the music faded out and a siren rang through the speakers. The group stopped dancing as a monotone message was out through the speakers "The police of Orange County are on the lookout for a criminal who avoided authorities two nights ago. He is believed to be a middle aged man who is roaming the Forest of Crystal Cove National Park. He is believed to be heavily armed and very dangerous. If anyone has any information on this man, they should contact the state police at…" Jack had reached in and shut the radio off, saying "We don't need to be focusing on that shit. We deal with demons and other bad mojo, not bad humans." The others nodded their agreement. Yet on the horizon, a dark line of clouds rolled in across the clear blue sea.

Chapter Two: Weird things, Freaky things.

After the sun had begun to set beyond the horizon, the group broke apart shortly. Jack and Serenity went to the local store to pick up some firewood. Mike and Jeff started digging up a fire pit, while Jas went strolling up and down the beach, searching for shells to use for necklaces.

As she strolled up and down the beach, listening to the boys laugh and throw sand at each other, she shook her head and mumbled "That pit's never gunna get dug at this rate." Suddenly, she felt something hit her foot. Looking down, she caught the glint of something buried in the sand. Bending down, she scooped it up, thinking it was a hermit crab or an especially shiny shell. When she brushed and blew the sand off, she was taken aback by the metal charm that sat in her palm.

She held it with great hesitation as she could feel some sort of energy ebbing and flowing through the red stone, just waiting to be released. Her fingers delicately traced the golden veins that laced through the silver. She wrapped the jewel in a protective ward to keep the energy from seeping into her before she went and washed her hands in the sea, muttering a small cleansing spell as she did it. As the spell went to take hold, the gem began sparking slightly. Disturbed, she walked back to the camp, wondering what she had just uncovered.

Meanwhile, Jack and Serenity were cruising up and down the streets of the town, looking for a store that sells bundles of firewood. As they drove, Serenity looked at Jack and said "Baby, when should we tell them about our... plans?" She rubbed her finger, where her ring usually sat. Jack shrugged his shoulders and replied "I really don't care honey, you were the one who wanted to wait for it."

"I just don't want them to judge us for it."

"They won't, I promise you that." Jack's eyes scanned around the small town, looking for the store. She continued "I just…I'm worried about what will happen when we tell people." Jack cut her off by placing his hand on hers and saying "Baby, you need to relax." His blue eyes sparkled as he continued, "With Grandpa's death and your family's' denouncement of us, this family is the only real one we've got left. They will be happy for us." Despite herself, she allowed a ghost of a smile to appear on her lips as she sighed and said "Ok baby."

Meanwhile, back on the beach, Jas was sprawled out on the bench and running string through some shells that she managed to dig up. As she ran the string through each shell, she whispered a soft spell, which made a small hole through the next one in the line. A passing thought told her to string the gem she discovered into the necklace, but she shook it away and kept going. As she worked with the shells, Mike and Jeff sat at the rustic table, playing a game of go fish with a deck of playing cards.

As the day fell to twilight, an itching sensation had crawled its way up Jas's neck and into the back of her mind. Feeling watched, she looked around their small spot of beach. Seeing no figures in the shadow, she mumbled a small spell under her breath. After only moments of stillness, a cold wind blew toward an area of trees that lined a portion of their campsite. Without thinking, her hand dropped to the small pouch that she had put the charm in, making sure it wasn't drawing anything to them and the ward was still in place. A slight movement in the trees threw her into high alert. Her eyes scanned the tree line with new intensity as her whispered voice said "I don't think we're alone."

Mike's sharp hearing picked up her words as he turned to her. Raising an eyebrow, he asked "Jas, honey, are you ok?"

She made a quick hand gesture and Mike caught her meaning. He nodded toward Jeff, who swiftly scooped up the cards and put them back in the small box. Then they both wandered over to her, keeping a look of casualness. When they were close enough, Mike whispered "What's the alarm?"

Jas said nothing, but motioned with her head toward the trees. Mike and Jeff both looked toward the trees. Jeff's golden eyes kept a constant sweep over the line as he whispered "Draw the circle, I'll keep my eyes peeled."

Keeping a cautious eye toward the trees, Jas and Mike began drawing in the sand, their practiced hands weaving the glyphs and symbols with quickened ease. Soon, they had a circle large enough to encompass the truck, their bonfire site, and the entire pack. As Mike sat with his legs crossed, stair at the trees, Jas turned her head to the north sky and called out "Spirits of protection, hear me. I fear darkness and evil this night. Mother Earth, bless our circle of protection and keep us safe." The wind softened and the stars sparkled a bit brighter, which put her mind at ease.

Meanwhile, Jack and Serenity were making their way out of the store, each weighed down by a couple bundles of fire wood in their arms. They had just checked out and walked through the doors when they heard a commotion. Ears perking up, Jack and Serenity put the wood in his truck and walked around to the back of the store to find a couple of teenagers harassing an older man. Light glinted off the teenager's jeans and chains. Both were clad in black tee-shirts, with baggy pants. One looked to be seventeen, while the other looked to be about fifteen to sixteen years old. The older one's hair was close cut, while the younger one's hair was shaggy and dyed a bright red. The man looked to be in his late sixties, with a scraggly beard and balding head. He was clad in an old leather jacket and blue jeans, but Jack could tell that he was hurting. He walked with a limp as he tried to go around the young teenagers that stood in his way. Jack's anger sparked as he saw the older one knock all the groceries out of the old gentleman's hands, sending all the items scattering along the ground. Jack had finally had enough as he barked out, "Hey! Knock that shit off."

The two teens turned and snarled at him. Jack cringed inwardly at the older one's face, which looked like it was repeatedly broken in several places. The youngher one wasn't much better, but he did have clear blue eyes, like Jacks. The older of the two sneered "What's this, some pussy thinkin' he's tough shit for his girly-friend?" They both started laughing, and Jack retorted, "Why don't you fight someone your own size, you ignorant bastards?" He had moved his hand behind his back and lighting began sparking between his fingers, the sparks arching from finger to finger. The thugs started moving away from the elderly man and spread out, intending to take them one-on-one. The smaller one drew a knife and smiled, revealing rows of teeth that, while white, had some gaps and jags, indicating more than a few broken teeth. He gestured to Serenity and said, "When we're done with you, we may get your girl there to spread and show us a good time. You want that, you little bitch?" He felt the familiar power growing and lurking behind his eyes, he looked at Serenity, only to see that same power slide it's self behind her eyes as well. He swallowed back and thought *"I can deal with this myself big guy, you're ok."* While no response came back, the prescience receded.

Serenity looked at them as her normally bright green eyes became a dark shade of pine. Calmly, she said "I'm sorry, but I don't do that for anybody." Her fists clenched and she locked her jaw. Jack saw this and he smiled a dangerous smile. Looking at the thugs, he started chuckling and asked "So, do you boys believe in magic?" The lighting cackled in his hand now, forming a ball of hot plasma in his palm. The bigger of the two sneered and said "What? You gunna disappear on your bitch?"

"No. I'm going to make you two disappear."
Jack whipped his hand around and cast the lighting
at the bully. Frightened, the older thug dove down to
the concrete, the ball of lightening just barely
missing his head. It was Jack's turn to sneer as he
said "What am I doing, I don't need magic to beat
you." He strode to the downed teen and he lifted
him to his feet, before a thunderous uppercut sent
him back to the ground. The smaller one paled and
looked toward Serenity, his mouth hanging opened
and his eyes wide. She smiled and nodded, saying
"Yes, *This Bitch*," putting emphasis on those two
words, "can do that too." She thrust her hand before
her and within seconds, heavy wind had slammed
into the teen's chest, sending him flying against a
telephone pole a few feet away from them. He slide
down the pole and sat there, attempting to catch his
breath. As he tried to stand, the winds hit him again,

pinning him in place. The larger teen managed to get back to his feet; and he and Jack were circling each other. After a few seconds, he yelled out and rushed Jack, fist raised to strike. With one fluid, practiced motion, Jack sidestepped the boy and wrapped his wiry arms around his throat. Jack then took all his weight and his muscle and forced it downward, dragging the teen down with him. Jack then kicked his legs out behind him and sat there, holding the teen in the chokehold, with his face buried just behind his neck to prevent any damage from his flailing arms. When he grew tired of holding him in place, Jack jumped off and summoned winds of his own.

In unison, Jack and Serenity lifted their targets up and threw them away. They landed together against a semi-truck trailer with enough impact to dent it. When they managed to pick themselves up, they turned and ran away screaming. Jack rushed to the old man's side, and helped him to his feet. Brushing him off, he asked "Are you ok sir? Do you need to go to the hospital?"

"No son, I'm fine. Thank you for your help." The old man went to grab his groceries, only to find Serenity had scooped them up and was already handing them to him. "We're sorry they attacked you. What did they want?"

The old man smiled warmly at her and said "Oh, money I suppose. People round this town are getting on hard times. Thing's ain't been the same since the fishin' went belly up."

Jack looked at him and asked, "What do you mean? We saw plenty of boats out in the cove."

"That may be, but they don't catch nothing. See, the boats go out every day, drag their nets cross the floor, but always come up empty handed. It's like all the fish just up and left the cove." Jack looked at Serenity and raised his eyebrow in question. She met his eye and asked the old man, "What happened?"

The old man scratched his beard for a bit, then answered "Well, some say it was a chemical spill or oil leak, but I'm not so sure. It seems kind of strange because there aren't any dead fish or anything else." He looked around and leaned in to them, whispering "Personally, I think there's something else going on, something that the normal folks don't see." His eyes took that sparkle as they sharpened. He whispered "Hunt well, you two. For something evil stalks the land." With that, the sparkle left and the man returned to normal.

Serenity looked at Jack, whose eyes showed the same feeling that stirred in Serenity's mind. She then said to the old man, "We need to get back to our friends and our camp. I hope you have a good day." The old man smiled again and he reached out and grabbed their hands, shaking them vigorously. He thanked them consistently, which they returned and smiled. When they finally extracted themselves from his grip, they walked back to their truck. As Jack opened the driver side door, he said "I wonder what is going on."

Serenity's response was a bit more animated "Was he one of us?! What did he mean 'Normal Folks'? What happened?" She went to get in the truck, then looked behind them to make sure that the old man wasn't standing there or following them.

Jack shut the door and stuck the key into the ignition. Once the engine started up, he responded "I don't know sweetheart. It's possible, but it's equally possible that he didn't know he was possessed or he was just a seer. You know, a human who can see us, feel us, that kinda stuff."

Serenity sighed and said "I guess so. All I know something strange is happening around this town, and I've got a bad feeling that we're gunna be swept up in it before long." Jack said nothing more, but he nodded and threw the truck in reverse, stomping on the gas. In the back of his mind, he had a funny feeling that she was right.

Back at camp, Mikey was getting impatient. "They should've been back by now." He was pacing the rim of the circle and looking at his phone. "They've been gone for over two hours. Something's happened, I just know it."

Jasmine looked at him and said reassuringly, "Calm down honey. It's probably nothing. They probably got lost." Jeff was leaning against the table, and he was looking toward the tree line. His piercing golden eyes scanning all along the thickest brush line. His voice was gravely and grim as he asked "What was the thing you found?"

Jas replied "The spell didn't tell me. It just revealed the thing's hiding spot."

He groaned, clearly displeased with the answer. His golden eyes continued to scan the tree line, looking for any signs of unnatural movement. His muscles tensed at every slight sound.

Jas, finally getting tired of Mike's pacing, got up and pulled him by the shoulders "Get a grip on yourself big guy. They are fine." He let out a deep breath, and looked into her eyes. Sighing, he reluctantly agreed "Yeah, they can handle themselves." Suddenly, Jeff dove down, hitting the sand and he yelled "Get down!"

They quickly dove as a sudden ball of fire energy splashed across their protective shield. When the fire dissipated, Jasmine hopped to her feet and raised her palms up above her head, summoning up a ball of light. Preparing to return fire, she yelled at Jeff, "Where the fuck did that come from?" Jeff pointed and sent a golden flare in the direction of the trees. Another dark ball of fire came from the tree line. When it hit the shield, the group gasped as it began to crack the shield. Whipping her arm around, she cast the ball of white light back toward the tree line. As she conjured up another, Jasmine turned to Mike and yelled "Use your energy to reinforce that damn barrier! I don't want this shield coming down around us down!"

Mike nodded and he summoned his hammer to his outstretched hand. Turning its head down, he planted it in the sand and began to chant. As he worked, tendrils of energy left the hammer and connected to the shield, fixing the breaks and bracing it.

Turning her attention back to the direction of their mystery attacker, Jas saw the headlights of an unknown vehicle driving down the beach, heading right for their camp. She sent a flare toward the vehicle, hoping to alert the driver and get them away. The light sparkled against shields that lined the vehicle, and Jas breathed a sigh of relief as she realized it was Jack's truck.

The truck drifted and turned to the side, skidding along in the sand and finally came to a stop on the outside of the circle. The driver side door flew open, and Jack rolled out into the circle, followed closely by Serenity. They ducked down behind the truck and looked to Jas, waiting for her to open the shield. Jas looked to Jeff, saying "Lay down covering fire. I don't want a lucky shot hitting home while I get those two to safety." Jeff nodded his understand and rose to his full height. He opened his hands and closed his eyes, forming football shaped balls of energy, each pulsing with a deep red glow. He raised his hands above his head and nodded to Jas, who began lifting the shield up. Jeff then hurled the two energy clustered toward the trees. Both clusters began to break into smaller balls of energy as they flew, effectively putting down a carpet bomb effect along the entire tree line. As they struck, Jas lifted the shield. When the hole was big enough, Serenity and Jack both rolled underneath. When they were clear, Jas let the shield back down and Jack sprung to his feet, hands open. The lightening cackling back to life in his palms. Looking around the group, he barked out, "Status report, now!"

Jas replied "We came under fire from a strange force, hitting us with enough firepower to crack our shield."

Jack smashed his hands together, and separated them, leaving a chain of lightening between the balls of energy. He threw them like a discus and sent them twirling toward the tree-line. The lightening exploded as it made contact with the trees, causing the tree line to burst into flame.

As he charged up another attack, a wall of fog emerged from the trees and encircled the group's position. Jack looked at Serenity, who shrugged her shoulders and said, "Don't look at me babe, this is a black fog. Besides, why would I want to mess with our vision?" Jack and Jas looked into the fog, trying to see past it. It was a thick, black mist that clung to the circle and to itself, making it nearly impossible to see through. Then, just as soon as it had come, the fog dissipated, leaving thin black ribbons of smoke to drift away in the wind.

Jack looked at Mike, pointed to the burning tree line, and said "You and Jeff try to get over there. I'm going to call up a storm to suppress the fire and cover your scents. Move slow, we don't know if that thing is still out there. " Jas took Serenity and said "We'll go around the flank, see if it's trying to run." Jack nodded his head and walked to the truck. He reached in the toolbox and pulled out a long staff, carved of oak. He muttered "Good thing I enchanted this to hold our gear." Twirling his custom mage's staff in his hands, he called up a storm to put out any smoldering fires and nodded to Mike, who lifted his hammer from the ground. He walked over next to jack and pulled his brother's twin headed battle axe from the box. He tossed Jeff his axe, saying "Let's go bro."

Jeff nodded and they both settled into a low crouch, moving as silently as they could. By now, the rains were falling heavily and the fire was smoldering out, reducing the light. They moved low, keeping their heads ducked down but always watching the line, anticipating another attack. Jas unraveled her whip and Serenity unsheathed her dagger. When they were ready, they moved around the back of the truck, mimicking Mike and Jeff's movements. They turned and headed back, almost parallel to the boys, but further inland, attempting to catch any fleeing demons. Jack meanwhile remained in the circle, keeping the storm centered over the tree line to obscure their various movements.

As they moved closer, a chilling laugh came from the smoldering brush. The four hunters slowed their approach to crawls. Eyes darted, grips tightened, all readied themselves for an attack that could come from anywhere, seen or unseen. Mike was the first to reach the brush line where the attack began. Picking his way around the dying flames and charred ground, he moved slowly. Jeff soon appeared on his right, he whispered, "Where did it go?" Mike scanned the ground, but found no tracks: coming or going. His head shook in intense, short motions, his unease clear. He turned his head to his far right, where the girls were hunting by the trails. Pursing his lips, he whistled a low, slow whistle to the girls, then crouched back down, waiting for the response.

Meanwhile, Jas and Serenity stalked near the foot of a medium sized hill, which was the only trail to that area. Serenity knelt to the wet ground and began muttering a spell designed to detect the use of stealth magic and the trail of demons. Jas's ears perked up upon hearing the signal. She responded with a whistle of her own. She then looked down at Serenity and said, "I've got nothing. Maybe this creature got hit and dissipated?" Nodding her agreement, Serenity stood back up and looked back at Jack, then over at Jeff and Mike. All the while, Jack's storm rained down, washing away the fire and all evidence.

Just as they were about to head back, the laugh was heard again, but quieter. This time, after the laugh had finished, a voice said "You think you have won, you believe all is grand, but take it from Freak, you'll die where you stand."

Jack swiftly called a retreat, as the pack began running back to the truck and the shield of Jack's staff and Jasmine's circle. Diving into it, Jeff looked up and said "Damnit Jack, where the fuck is he?! I can't fight an enemy when I've got no fucking clue where he is!" Jack held up has hand for silence, then he looked at Serenity and said, "Call forth the wind, I have something to say." At a motion of her hand and a hum of her voice, Jack's booming message ringed throughout the country side "I go by many names: Wizard and Mage, Striker, Alpha, Vulcanos. But whatever you wish to call me demon, hear these words. We will not die to the likes of you, coward. You, who dare not face us in open combat, you who hide and slaughter innocent people. We will find you, Nameless One, and we will send you back to whatever foul abyss that you crawled out of." Once he finished, he raised his voice in a vicious war howl, which was quickly joined by the group. One by one, they raised their voices and let the wind carry their combined howl to wherever the demon lay.

When the howls had been carried away, and the wind died, the group stood motionless and silent. After a few moments, Jack sighed and said "So much for a fucking vacation." Every member of the group nodded and muttered their agreement.

Serenity looked at Jack, her face lit up as she made the connection. She asked "What if this demon is responsible for all the fish leaving? Maybe the negative energy is poisoning the earth." Jack rubbed his small goatee, a low hum came from his throat as he thought about her words. Eventually, he nodded his agreement, saying "It's very possible. After all, we've seen it before. Demons come in, then the natural energy of the place goes out." Sighing, he rubbed his temples with his index and middle fingers, then said "Look, it's too dangerous for us to sleep out in the open. I say we fall back and try to find somewhere indoors to stay." Mike pointed back toward the main highway and said "When we were coming in, I saw a hotel just outside of town. Maybe they could have some rooms left?"

The group began breaking down the site: Jas removed her circle from the sand, Serenity and Jack loaded the weapons back into the toolbox and locked it. All the while Mike and Jeff stood, watching for any more attacks. Once the site was cleared and cleaned, they all piled in: Jack and Serenity took the driver and passenger seats, Jeff took the back seat behind the driver, Jas took the center seat and Mike sat behind Serenity. When they started to pull away, Jeff put his hand outside the window and muttered a quick spell. Almost immediately, Jack's truck was surrounded by a shimmering, glowing mist. Rolling the window up and nodding to Jack, he laid his head on the head rest and closed his eyes. Jas put her head on Mike's shoulder, which caused him to wrap his arm around her and rub her shoulder. In the front, Serenity scooted into the middle seat next to Jack and started to sing softly. Jack's grip on the wheel loosened as one of his hand's let go and grasped hers. Glancing over, he met her eyes briefly and allowed a smile to show. From the back, Jeff said "Hey Serenity, you have an amazing voice and all, but I'm trying to recover back here."

Serenity shrugged and replied "Just trying to lighten the mood bro, sorry."

With that, the car fell silent again.

Chapter Three: Know Thy Enemy

The truck was quiet as they reached the hotel. Jack smoothly pulled into the blacktop lot from the road. He pulled into the small driveway by the front door to let Serenity out. Serenity slid out of her seat to go inside and collect their keys, as she had called ahead to get two adjoining rooms so the pack could stay. Serenity ran inside to check them in and grab the keys while Jack said, "Alright, you guys know the drill: Go in, purify the room completely, and set up defenses. I don't wanna get caught with our pants down again." All he got was half asleep murmers in response. Serenity got back in the truck and guided Jack to a parking spot by a small side door, where they could slip in and out of their room without much notice. They then filed out of the car, with Mike, Jeff and Jack going to the bed of the truck while Jas and Serenity went inside. Mike and Jack pulled out two black duffle bags each, while Jeff had one. Jeff yawned as he moved ahead of Jack to grab the door that Serenity held open.

The group walked to the elevator and Serenity said "We are on the second floor, rooms 201 and 203. They are adjoined, just as I requested." She handed Mike and Jas their key and held on to her and Jack's. Calling the elevator, Jeff said "I hope this place is safe. I'd feel better if civi's weren't caught in the crossfire."

"I wonder if it was behind that attack by those two boys that we heard about over the radio." Jack thought aloud.

"Could be," replied Jasmine, "It certainly does seem strange that it's here at all."

Mike was quiet for a time, then he chimed in, "What if it's looking for something? Or someone?

Maybe it was stolen from and it's looking to get it back." Mike's comment jogged Jas's memory as she pulled out the small pouch. As she tugged on the draw string she said "Let's get in the room." Curiosity drew the others into Jack and Serenity's room behind her, with Jeff shutting the door behind them. When the door was shut and secured, she turned around, revealing the jewel. The other's looked at it with mixed expressions while she explained "I found it while I was scouting the beach, looking for shells. I can feel an old, mysterious energy pulsating and swirling in the gem." She gave it to Jack, who had immediately held his hand out to examine it. When it landed in his palm, his face fell into an expression of wonder, but also suspicion. As he handed it Serenity, he said "I assume you warded this thing. It seems like it's…"

Jeff cut him off "FUCK!" He dropped it from his hand and grabbed his wrist. On his palm was a burn: Perfectly circular and the exact size of the gem. Serenity immediately began cleaning his wound as Jas said "I warded that thing off from Demon's and dark energy."

Jack turned and looked at Jeff, worry flashing across his eyes as he quietly said "Jeff, your necklace, where is it?"

With his free hand, Jeff pulled out the small, bronze coin from around his neck. Jack lifted it carefully and examined the metal, before returning it to him and nodding. They ignored the various looks of confusion from the group as Jack looked back to Jas and said "It seems like the energy from the ring is alive. It's reacting to different people differently." He nodded over at Jeff and continued "When I held it, the energy seemed to retreat further into the gem, yet it burns Jeff when he touches it."

Mikey looked at the small piece of jewelry and growled slightly, muttering "That damn thing better watch itself."

Jas scooped it back up and returned it to the pouch, saying "Like I said, I found it on the beach. I don't know where it came from."

Jack thought for a moment, then he said "Until its purpose is discovered, keeping it locked away might be the best course of action."

The group nodded and Jack sighed heavily, continuing "Guys it's been a long day. Let's purify the rooms, set up our wards, and then get to sleep. We'll get up early, get some of that free breakfast, and then meet back here to plan." Nodding, the group disappeared to begin their rituals.

Jack set their bags on the floor, just at the foot of the bed and Serenity got out her purification kit; a small wand made of dried sage leaves, and a lighter filled with natural oils. She clicked the lighter's switch, and watched as the small flame danced to life. As she put the fire to the tip of the wand, she began to sing. Her voice rose and fell in a soft Irish melody. Once the tip of the wand caught flame, she released the switch and let the fire retreat back into the lighter. Her song became a homemade purification spell as she shook the fire out, leaving the dried leaves smoldering, releasing a pure white smoke. Chanting the spell, she walked slowly around the room and let the smoke dance around the bed, windows, and throughout the room. The soft, white smoke settled into the furniture and air, burning away the negative energy.

While she did this, Jack removed a leather bound book, a sketch pad, and a graphite pencil. He settled at the desk in the room and began flipping through the pages of the book. After a few moments of flipping, he settled on an old set of Nordic runes, used for protection. With a swift, practiced hand, he drew several of the symbols onto different sheets of paper. As he drew, he muttered a spell of his own make, designed to infuse the symbols on the paper with energies of safety and protection.

When he was satisfied with the look of the runes, he tore out the pages and set them in various points around the room. He placed them at each corner of the door, along the window sills, and he even put one below each of the vents, making impossible for negative energy to come into the room. In short order, the protection was laid down and the room was clean. Sighing, Jack looked at

Serenity and said "I'm going to go take a hot shower, I need to wash off and relax." Serenity laid down on the bed and turned on the T.V. Flipping through channels, she said "Ok honey, I'll be waiting right here." She smiled softly and blew him a kiss before settling on an old re-run of NCIS.

Jack stepped into the bathroom and shut the door. Sighing, he turned on the facet and let the water run into the rather long tub while he shed his black shorts and his old tie-dye tee-shirt. He stood in his boxer briefs, and enjoyed a few moments of quiet. As those moments past, he walked to the mirror and met his own gaze.

He shook his head as he forced himself to recognize how much toll his life had taken upon his body: His eyes started to sink into his skull, his beard had begun to grow grey hairs, and his irises lost much of their blue sparkle. His skin became pale, his once strawberry blonde mane of hair had grown flat and some lines of silver even shown there. Bowing his head, he whispered, "How can one person age this much in such a short time? Has my leadership taken that much of a toll on me?" He looked at his reflection again. He ran his eyes down his body, and smiled slightly. While his face had revealed his tired expression, his body still bore the toned, defined arms and chest, bore from a life of work and struggles. The scars from his many battles were still defined against his skin, and the tattoos that crossed his body still held their bright colors and defined lines. He raised his arms and flexed, letting his favorite piece catch the light: It was a well-wrote half sleeve, adorned with hard tribal edges that formed a wolf's paw, caressing his shoulder. The brilliant silver and the deep blue danced together throughout the piece. He smiled at it, then he reached down to his side and touched his first. A small robin that flew across his left side, just under his heart. Tears filled his eyes as the memories came again.

He was standing by an old, leather reclining chair, where an old man lay dying. A soft voice says "Jack, come closer." The young man knelt by the chair and said through a choked voice "I'm here grandpa."

The voice said again "Give me your hand, Jack. I want to give you" a shuddering breath interrupted the sentence "a passing gift."

Jack turned his hand up to his grandfather, who placed a carved wooden owl in his hand. With a smile he said "Remember, at the end of all lives, we've gotta test to take. This will be on it." They both laughed at the old joke as Jack said, tears forming in his eyes "You'll beat this grandpa. I know you will. You're so strong." The old man placed a hand on his cheek and said "I can hear the spirits calling me home." Seeing his grandson's tears rolling down his cheek, his grandfather wiped them away and said softly, "Remember me like I was. Hiking through the trails and loving the world." His chest shuddered as he said softly "Bye bye for now Jack." With that he closed his eyes and his chest fell still.

Jack jerked out of the memory as tears streamed down his face. Gasping for air, he forced himself to breath deep and focus. Recovering his composure, he lifted the tab on the tub faucet. A moment lapsed as the water went from pouring out from the main faucet in the tub, to spraying down from the shower head. He waited until the water began to steam before he stepped in. He leaned back under the shower head and let his long, strawberry blonde hair fall down his back, the water leaving trails of warmth as they fell through his hair and streamed down his arched torso. A smile playing on his face as he began to relax. He grabbed a washcloth from the rack and applied body wash to it. He lathered it up and started to whistle a soft tune as the door softly creaked open. Hearing it, he shrugged and kept whistling, wondering if his fiancé had decided to stop in and pay him a visit. A soft cough was heard as the door shut again, and through the translucent shower curtain, he saw the blurry outline of a figure standing in the bathroom. As the figure moved closer, Serenity's voice asked "Jack, honey, are you ok? I heard sobbing, followed by silence."

Jack let a sigh escape as he replied "I guess I'm ok now. Just got lost in memories." He sat down towards the front of the tub, the faucet gently pressing into his back.

"Would you like some company, sweetheart?"

"I'd like that."

Just as he expected, he saw Serenity's hand reach around and gently pull back the curtain. She stood before him in her favorite dark red swimming suit and looked at him. Her face adopted a sweet, caring smile as she stepped into the space he left open for her. She sat across from him, their knees touching as they tried to get comfortable. After a while, they stopped moving and just stared at each other, enjoying a comfortable silence. Jack was the first to break the silence as he sighed and said "I can't believe he's gone. Every day I look at this bird on my side and I have to convince myself that he isn't coming back." He bowed his head to hide the tears from his mate, who had reached across the water and put her hands on both his shoulders.

She held him there for a few moments, then she put one of her fingers on the underside of his chin and gently raised his head to meet her gaze, then she said "Jack, so long as we remember him, he will never truly be gone from this world. He lives on through our memories, our thoughts and actions. He lives on through the robin on your side and through Toby." Jack allowed a small smile as he thought back to the small, wooden owl that sits in their library, guarding their knowledge and watching them.

Seeing him smile, even though his eyes sparkled with tears, made Serenity smile as she continued "Even though his physical shell may be gone, his spirit remains with us."

Jack bobbed his head up and down, saying nothing. The silence returned for a moment, but then Jack wept. He wept for his departed grandpa, he wept for his broken family, and he wept for his lost mother. The tears that he couldn't shed in public fell in the comforting solitude that he shared with his mate. While he wept, Serenity said nothing, but shifted her position to one where she was on her knees. She took her weeping mate in her arms and held him close to her heart.

They sat like that for a while, and when Jack stopped crying, he pulled away slightly, looking Serenity in the eyes. Seeing his loving mate always made him smile. She stroked his hair, whipped away his tears with her thumb, and kissed his lips softly, causing them both to close their eyes and get lost in the moment. They held the kiss for a moment or two, and when they finally broke apart, he smiled back. As they showered, they spoke no more words, but shared a romantic time with each other.

As Jack reached over and turned the water off, Serenity broke the silence and asked, "So Alpha, where do we start hunting?"

Jack took a few seconds to think about it. He stepped out onto the cold tile floor and said "I was thinking we can have Jeff and Mike go back to the beach in the day time. Have them return to the spot of the ambush and see if we can gather any more intel. You and Jas can go track down the boy and see what he knows. I was going to go to the store and stock up on supplies and see what kind of local legends I can gather up." He held out a pristine white towel toward his mate, who stood still in the wet tub.

"Sounds good to me honey. I just hope we can catch this thing." She went silent again, stepping out of the tub. She reached out and took the proffered towel, but her face radiated with concern. As she wrapped the towel around her bathing suit, she asked, " Whatever that was...Was it natural to this world or do you think it would have to be created?

I'm only asking because we've been up against a lot: Necromancers, Hellhounds, Fallen angels." Jack's thoughts flashed back to Troy, when their family's first real battle.

Burning corpses in the fire place. Bodies cut and sewn back together again. Limbs hanging from meat hooks on the ceiling. In the center of it all stood a stone alter, blackened by hellfire. Behind it stood a tall, bulky man with dark hair and eyes, and beside him sat a large, black dog. The dog was easily the size of a young grizzly, with coarse black fur and blood red eyes. The claws and teeth were stained red from the blood of men. The man laughed as he wielded a butcher's knife with skill that can only be obtained with years of practice. Jack and the pack looked on in horror as the seemingly normal man grinned an evil grin and ripped out the heart of his latest victim.

In a sudden blur of movement, the man cut the chain that held the dog back. As the beast charged, the man ran with it, laughing and swinging the blade all about.

Jack broke the memory as Serenity continued "We've exorcised demons and broken oppressions. Yet, despite all our battles, all our adventures, I don't think we've ever stood against something that had that much power. I mean, it managed to avoid detection and still had energy enough to crack Jas's circle shield."

He sighed, then replied "I'm not sure. It could be a construct or it could be something more." He stopped, clearly distraught by the possibility. Then he continued "I don't care what this is. It's clearly up to no good and we need to put this beast down."

Serenity stared into his eyes as he spoke, the quiet passion in his voice stealing her breath away.

She smiled and she watched him wrap a towel around his lower half and walk out of the bathroom. Filled with desire, she shed her bathing suit and she walked out. Leaning against the doorframe, she shut off the light and whispered "Jack." When he turned around, she tackled him onto the bed, kissing him with fiery passion. Growling, Jack quickly rolled themselves to where he was topping. Planting his hands on either side of her body, he raised himself up and smirked "What, wanna try and tame this big dog again?" Serenity smiled and purred, "It isn't that hard. You become a puppy at my touch." The room filled with giggling as they turned out the lights.

The soft, golden light of the sun streamed into the window as it crested the horizon, signaling the dawn. As it fell onto Jack's sleeping face, he awoke to see Serenity curled against his chest, still asleep. Smiling down at her sleeping form, he gently kissed the top of her head and laid back, looking up at the ceiling. His eyes followed the swirling pattern that ringed the small ceiling fan. Its curves and ridges spiraled clockwise out from the center. As the seconds ticked by, Jack sank into a meditative trance, fading into his thoughts *"What are we up against? It's clearly something evil, and powerful. This entire town is suffering from it's simple existence, so what would happen if it decided to take a more active campaign against the people."*

His thoughts were broken as Serenity's breathing changed and she stirred against his chest. She looked up at him with a sleepy look and said, "Good morning honey." She raised her head and kissed his neck softly. There was no fiery passion in the kiss, but a gentle love for her mate and alpha. Jack looked back down at her and smiled. "Morning sleeping beauty. Did you have a good night's sleep?"

Smiling, she replied playfully "Every night is a good night's sleep when I work out before bed." She kissed his cheek and nestled into him, sighing with contentment as he pulled her closer to his chest, wrapping his arm around her shoulders. A sudden thud was heard next door, followed by a series of knocks. Jack looked at her and joked, "Sounds like the kids are up."

She started to pout. "I was comfy."

Kissing her nose, Jack smiled and said, "So was I, but we've got work to do." Jack slipped out of the bed and reached down to his duffle bag. Reaching in, he withdrew a pair of thin, black workout pants. As he stepped into them, Serenity took her clothes into the bathroom.

When she had closed the door behind her, and Jack had his pants on, he opened the door and was greeted by Mike's hand reaching around and slapping him in the back of the head. As Jack rubbed his head, he glared at Mikey, who looked back and said "Look, I don't care what you do in your bedroom, but when she's screaming so loud that it wakes us up, then it bugs me." Jack just smiled and shrugged his shoulders, replying, "Hey, I got lucky last night, so I really don't care." Jas shoved past them both and said "Yeah well, I really didn't need to hear how big your dick was and how good it felt." She shuddered as Jack laughed. Shaking his head, he looked past Mike into their room and asked "Aw well. Anyway, where's the other guy?" Mike gestured downstairs and replied "You know him: Up at five, in the weight room or gym by five thirty, breakfast whenever, then business. Speaking of which," Mike turned to Jas and said, "I think I'll go join him." He kissed her and continued "We'll meet you in the lobby at 8:30 for breakfast." He turned and headed out the door.

Serenity opened the bathroom door and gestured, "Put some clothes on fool." Before Jack could respond, Jasmine looked at her and said "It don't matter what he wears now, I already know what he's packing."

Serenity blushed bright red and said, "I-I'm sorry, I didn't realize I was that loud."

Jasmine shook her head and sighed, saying "Ah well, it doesn't matter now."

Jack retreated to the bathroom and Jas looked at Serenity and said "Hey, I've gotta question for you. It's about you and Jack." Serenity looked at her and she tilted her head slightly, asking "Yeah, What's up?" Jas strode to their bed and sat down. Crossing her legs, she asked "Is there something going on between you two?" At first, she was going to deny it, but a sudden wave of giddiness came over Serenity and she walked back over to her duffle bag. She reached down and pulled out the small velvet box. Looking at it, she sighed happily and said "Now that you mention it, there is something." She flipped open the box's lid, revealing a small ring. Serenity pulled the ring from the box and held it up in the light. Jas's eyes met a silver band with a decent size garnet set in the center, surrounded by smaller sapphires and rubies. Jasmine's jaw dropped as Serenity exclaimed "We're engaged!"

Jas sat there, speechless. She marveled at the ring and she looked at Serenity's face as it beamed with happiness. She got up and looked at the ring, sensing the enchantments on it right away. She looked at Serenity, who suddenly looked sad and worried. She said "I was scared to tell you guys because I didn't know what you all would think if we got engaged." Jas shook her head and slapped Serenity upside hers, saying "We're a pack dumbass. We support each other." Looking at the bathroom, she saw Jack emerging wearing his black cargo shorts and belt with a cut off black tank top. Walking over to him, she slapped him and said "The next time something big like that happens, I expect you to tell us you fool." She then hugged him tightly and said "Congratulations bro, I'm so happy for the both of you."

Jas walked back into her room. As the sounds of her rummaging through her duffle bag came into the room, Jack looked at Serenity, a knowing smile on his face. Jack then saw the ring sitting on her finger and said "You told her, didn't you." Serenity looked down sheepishly and replied "Yes I did." Jack smiled, then he walked over to her and wrapped his arms around her waist. In a sudden burst of movement, he lifted her up and twirled her around. When he put her down, they kissed. They held that position until Jasmine coughed and said "Look, I can shut this door if you guys need to deal with something." Looking at each other, Jack and Serenity laughed and Jas shook her head, mumbling "You're both nuts." She went back into her room and the next sound they heard was the bathroom door closing.

Jack looked at Serenity and said "Well, we might as well make the announcement to the pack. After all, they'll find out soon enough." Serenity nodded, kissed his nose one last time, and then she said "I'll get our gear ready." Prying herself from his arms, she walked over to their bag and knelt down. She opened a small, cushioned compartment that was hidden in the lining of the bag. She reached into the hidden section and began pulling out small, glass bottles of dried herbs; as well as five small, white metal cylinders. Checking the pins carefully, she removed them and said "These are freshly made. Just pull and throw. The smoke will do the rest." She then handed one to Jack, which he immediately put aside by his wallet and truck keys.

Once they had all the gear assembled and Jas was ready, they walked down from the room into the lobby.

They found Mike and Jeff had already found the dining area. They sat in a half circle booth, filling the corner closest to the buffet tables. The vinyl seats were bright red and shiny, as they reflected the lights in the ceiling. The smell of fresh cooked bacon and eggs waffled through the air. Jack looked around and saw a mother of four trying to wrangle her brood and make them pick their breakfast, he saw a handful of other couples sitting at their tables, some were reading the newspaper or watching the weather channel on a TV that was mounted to the wall. He focused his energy on his own mind, keeping the outside energies from overwhelming his senses.

Walking over, Jas scooted in beside Mike and Jeff moved around the table to make room for Serenity and Jack. When everyone was seated at the table, Mike smiled at Jas, then said "Well, we got plates for you all but they went cold so we ate them." Patting his belly, he smiled, then let out a loud belch that caused two tables to pick up their plates and move, and a mother with four laughing kids to give him an icy glare. A smile played a crossed Jasmine's face as she said "Good one honey, but wait until I've had my coffee and bacon and we'll see who's got the better belch." They laughed as Jack shook his head and said "I don't know about the rest of you clowns, but I am getting something to eat." Serenity smiled and batted her eyelashes, saying "Can you get me some too baby?" Jack rolled his eyes and smiled, then he slid out from the booth and walked toward the buffet, grabbed two plates as he passed by the china table.

As he walked away, he heard Jeff whispered "Whipped." He smiled and mouthed a spell under his breath, waited a few seconds and then turned his back just in time to see Jeff start itching behind his left ear. Chuckling to himself, he returned to the buffet and started filling the plates: He filled his plate with eggs, bacon, sausage, and a doughnut; while Serenities plate got a banana, some grapes, two biscuits, some eggs and a glass of juice.

While he was gone, Serenity told the rest of the group everything: Their vacation to Colorado, the rainstorm that stranded them in the hotel, and finally the romantic night when Jack proposed. When she pulled out the ring, Mike and Jeff hooted their congratulations and then immediately began fighting over who their first kid what going to be named after.

When Jack returned with the food, the noise only got louder as they both fought for his opinion. He put Serenity's food in front of her and he said "We've already got names picked out for our kids guys, don't worry." Serenity started devouring her food as Jack sat down and began eating his own food. The bacon disappeared from both their plates within seconds, followed by the eggs. Serenity was picking at her grapes and sipping at her juice when Jack pushed his plate to the side and said "Now, let's get down to business."

"To defeat the huns?" Mikey and Jeff giggled at the joke. However, their laughter stopped when Jack glared at them and their faces sobered.

The group leaned in as Jack laid out the plan "Alright guys, we're going to have to split up to cover the ground and figure out what exactly is going on: Jeff, you and Mike are going to the beach to see if you can pick up on anything that may still be there: Footprints, scents, anything. Jasmine and Serenity are going to track down the boys from the attack a few nights back and see if they are related in any way. I'm going to go to the store and pick up some supplies to stock our supplies, and see if I can talk up some of the locals." He looked around, then whispered, "We have some purification bombs ready if we need to use them. One for each of us, so use them wisely. When we're all finished eating, we will return to the room as a group. Then I will leave first, followed by Jas and Serenity. Mike, I want you two to go out the back so it still seems like there is someone in the room. Remember to arm our defenses and take it slow. We meet at the Sonic on Main Street for lunch, but I want everyone reporting in every hour or so and we meet back here to compare at three. If you don't show, we go out hunting." They all muttered their agreement and the rest of breakfast past quickly. After the meeting, Jasmine got up and retrieved her own breakfast, which consisted of cereal, a muffin, and some fruit.

In short order, the team returned to the room and donned there gear: Mike changed out of his sweatpants and old tee-shirt, in favor of his blue jeans and a crisp, white tee-shirt which was covered by a dark leather jacket. Jeff had a pair of camouflaged shorts and a grey tank top. Jasmine adorned a collection of bracelets, each one enchanted to block enemy attacks and help her own hit home. Her main attire was a pair of black skinny jeans and a tight black tee shirt. The finishing touch was her black shades and a baseball cap, with her long red hair sticking out through the back. Serenity donned a tie-die tank top and a pair of denim, carpi shorts. Crossed her waist went a white, leather belt, adorned with a belt buckle that had a segment missing from the center. She wore shades of her own, but hers weren't the dark tint that Jas's were.

Jack handed Serenity and Jasmine his truck keys, claiming he could walk to the store and walk back. Mike and Jeff agreed to be picked up a couple blocks away at the gas station. Jack looked at his pack and said "Be safe you guys, we've got no idea where this thing is coming from or what it wants." The team nodded and Jack went to walk out the door. He stopped to get his staff, which he had leaned against the door. He quickly made into a common walking stick, thanks to his illusion magic.

As he walked out the lobby door, he cast one last look at the hotel and he whispered "Goddess Nyx, Queen of the night and our loving protector, watch over my pack as we hunt this day in your holy name. Blessed be." With that, he squared his shoulders and whistled a tune as he walked off into the town.

As he walked away, Jasmine looked at Serenity and said "Alright sister, let's move out." She turned and kissed Mike goodbye as he handed her the whip, which transformed into a cloth belt that she deftly looped through her pants. Serenity's dagger shrunk down and she slid it into the slot on her belt buckle, leaving the hilt in a position where she could easily draw it. They walked out and started talking loudly, making it known that they were leaving. Getting into the truck, Jasmine sent a text to Mike, saying "At the truck, make your move." Putting her phone in her pocket, she looked at Serenity and asked "Any ideas?"

Looking out the window, Serenity thought for a moment. Finally she said "My guess would be the local hospital. It seems like the child may have been admitted after the attack. At least, it makes the most sense." Nodding her agreement, Jas started the truck and made for the rendezvous point to meet with Mike and Jeff.

Meanwhile, Mike and Jeff finished locking up the rooms and walked. Mike summoned a shadowy veil to conceal them from view as they made their way down the stairs, towards a side door, both looked to the ground and had to make conscious effort in placing there steps, trying to make as little noise as possible. When they were out of the hotel and a decent distance down the street, Mike took down the shadow wall and they walked toward the Shell station. As they waited for the girls (who decided to circle the block a couple times) Mike said to Jeff "Ain't no rest for the wicked, eh brother?" Jeff laughed and he started twirling his axe, which he concealed into a cane-like walking stick. The clack of the black wooden cane striking the concrete was the only sound for a time. Mike looked to his little brother as they walked and sighed. He could see the nervousness was plain on Jeff's face as he asked "Bro, do you think that someone may die from this? I mean, what kind of creature has the power to crack one of Jas's shields? She has some of the strongest powers in our group." Mikey reached over and hit his brother upside his head while saying "Don't ever talk like that. We're not going to die here or anywhere else alright?" He looked hard into his brother's eyes until he nodded and sighed "Thanks bro."

Just then, they both heard the low rumble of the truck's engine as they saw the black pick up pull into the shell's lot. Serenity rolled down the window and made a small gesturing motion to the back seat, saying "Alright boys, let's get moving." Mike and Jeff climbed into the back and they were off.

Meanwhile, Jack was walking around the small grocery store that he and Serenity were at yesterday. He browsed the aisles, trying to seem inconspicuous and listen to local talk. So far, all he knew was who was sleeping with who and who was thrown in jail. He was about to give up and pay for the bottle of coke that he was carrying with him, when he heard an old man say "I wonder what's causing these strange happenings? It's not like the animals to just spook like that."

Another voice replied "Yeah, well I don't know either. Last night round midnight they all started kicking up and making all kinds of noise out in the barn."

"Did a rat or possum get in there?"

"Not that I saw. Just the horses and the goats. I thought I saw someone run out but when I went looking in the field, I didn't see any footsteps. Called the sheriff but he couldn't see anything either." Jack had settled into an aisle full of candies and large two liters to listen in. The voices came up from the aisle next to him again "I don't know. But I went out on the boat this morning, the lake seemed different. It looked greenish, like it was sick. I got a fish but he was a weird color and he didn't put up much of a fight, so I threw him back."

"Hm, seems like everything's gone to hell around here: Fishin's gone, animals are getten sicker and sicker, and I've even noticed some fokes been acting a little oddly."

"How do ya figure?" At this point, Jack's interest was through the roof

The old man was quiet for a time, then his voice dropped low "I saw Ms. Summers, standin' out in the middle of Willow's cemetery, all by her lonesome. I was going to go up and ask if she was alright, until I noticed that she was smiling. Not one of her pretty white smiles, neither. Her smile was twisted and evil, like the devil himself was in her."

An audible gulp was heard, then the other fellow replied "I don't know. But now that you mention it, I went to see Doc Johnson the other day and he was acting real goofy. Kept asking me if I was baptized yet or if I needed healen. I kept asking him why he was wonderen, but all he did was laugh at me. Didn't even seem to notice when I left his office."

"Ah well, I'm sure everything will be alright in the end. Usually is. So, how's your daughter liken school out east?"

"She's doin' well, made the dean's list..." After that, it became clear that they had talked enough, and Jack was ready to go.

As he paid for the soda, the cashier took one look at him and said "You're not from around here, are ya son." Sensing it wasn't a question, he replied "No, I'm from out east a ways." He picked up his bag and turned to leave, but the man grabbed his wrist, his eyes grew wild and he whispered "Get outta town stranger, and don't stop runnin'. There's some weird things happening, and it's going to get people killed, you mark my words." Jack wore a calm face, but his guts were churning inside. He firmly broke the grasp that the cashier had on him and whispered back "What do you mean?" But the cashier's eyes returned to normal as he said "You have a nice day now. " Jack didn't stay to ask any more questions, he turned on his heel and left the store.

Jas and Serenity pulled into the hospital parking lot after dropping off Mike and Jeff at the beach. They got out and looked up at the three floor building. Eventually, Serenity looked at Jas and said "I'll see if we can find the boy's room, you chat up some people. See what you can learn." Jas nodded and walked inside. Once they entered the lobby, they were hit by the smell of hospital: Disinfectant, Medicine, and the odor of sickness. Serenity looked at the map for the long term rooms as Jas walked up to the front desk. She leaned on her elbow, looking at the small man working the desk. She took a moment to size him up: Small, thin build, thinning hairline and wire frame glasses. He was staring intently at the computer, almost oblivious to the fact that she was there. Jasmine cleared her throat and asked "Excuse me sir, do you handle new admins at this desk?"

He didn't even look up as he answered "I do, please fill out this paperwork." His eyes briefly fell away from the computer as he reached below his desk and grabbed a clip board with medical questions and insurance questions. Jas chuckled as he put in in front of her, then she said "No, I'm from FBI. I'm here regarding the attack on the two children in the forest that occurred a couple nights ago."

That got his attention. He looked up from the screen as he asked replied "I.D?"

Jasmine looked at him for a moment, then she sighed and said "Fine." She dropped one hand below the desk and made the sign for confusion. Once she felt the magic take effect, she pulled her wallet out of her back pocket and flashed her license at him.

The receptionist blinked three times, then took off his glasses and rubbed his eyes, clearly not able to focus.

After a while, he shook his head and said "Alright, what would you like to know?"

Jasmine smiled slightly and replied "I was wondering if the boys were still in your care, and if so, I would like to speak to them."

"I'm afraid you're a little mistaken. There was only one boy in the hospital, the other one was found deeper in the woods. It was. . . " the man stopped, and cleared his throat "The EMT's couldn't revive him. His body was mangled beyond repair."

Jasmine nodded solemnly and said "I'm sorry; where is the survivor now?"

The man smiled slightly and said "Let me take a look." He turned his gaze back to the screen and typed in the query. After a couple moments of searching, he looked back up and said "I'm sorry, but it says here that he was released back home just earlier this morning. The damage wasn't too severe, so the doctor's signed the release."

Jasmine nodded her head and said "Thank you, sir. You've been very helpful." With that, she turned and signaled to Serenity, and they walked out the doors, back to the parking lot.

They got back into the truck and Jas looked at Serenity, then said "Well, this was a dead end. I hope the boys have better luck then we did."

Chapter Four: On the Hunt.

Meanwhile, on the beach, Jeff and Mike were looking at the land. The sand was black and brittle from the fires, the brush was chard and thin. They began picking through the remains, but they were having little luck in tracking the creature's movements. Jeff looked at the scorched land where Jack had set fire to the brush. He picked through the burnt landscape as he said "Bro, I don't think that we'll be able to find anything. I think Jack may have burned it all away. That, or he washed it away with the storm he conjured up." Mikey nodded his head and he replied "I agree with you there brother."

Suddenly, Jeff stopped and looked at a patch of dirt, saying, "Mike, look at this." He knelt down and read the ground, which slowly uncovered tracks. Mike wandered over and when he saw them, he gasped. They were at least a foot and a half in length, with five toes. What stuck out was that in front of each toe sat a small circular point that ran ahead about six inches from the main print. Mike cleared up the dirt with a spell and took his phone from his jacket. He flipped the edge up and opened his camera. A series of clicks followed as he snapped several pictures of the prints. Putting his phone back in his pocket, he asked "What do you think those are? Claw prints or talon markings?"

Jeff followed the trail and said "They lead into the hills." He gave his brother a devilish smirk and asked "Shall we go hunting, my brother?" Mike smiled and he shot Jack a quick text, saying what they found and that they were following it. When it sent, he uncloaked his hammer and Jeff summoned his axe. Jeff smiled as he said "The brothers are back on the hunt." With that, they took off down the trail, following the footprints into the hills and away from the beach.

Jack was back at the hotel, mixing the potions for the group to purify the area when he got the message. Cursing, he replied back "No, stay away until we are ready to hunt." When they didn't reply, he swore violently and called Serenity. She answered "Hey baby, we were about to check in. We're going to..."

Jack cut her off "Baby, Mike and Jeff ran off. They're chasing some set of tracks through the hills. I'm going in after them. Keep doing what you two are doing and check in with me every few minutes. If I go dark, go to the beach and look for the flare." She was silent, her gut twisted with nerves. She forced herself to breath, and then said "Happy hunting my love, be safe please. You've still gotta come back and marry me." That made him smile as he said "I will, I love you, goodbye baby." When she replied, he hung up and grabbed his weapons. Locking up the rooms, he took off.

Serenity hung up the phone and faced Jasmine, who looked on her with concern. Serenity said "Your man may be getting himself killed." Upon hearing that, she spun a violent U-turn, causing several drivers to honk and cuss. Speeding down the road to the beach, saying "What in the name of holy fuck is going on?"

"I don't know, Jack called saying that they ran off into the hills on the demons trail." Serenity clung to the handle above the door, silently praying that the goddess would shield her from this insane road rage. Jas flew off the handle and let loose a storm of cussing and rage that surprised even Serenity, as she hadn't really heard Jas get so upset. "That stupid mother fucker! What the fuck does he think he's doing going in there without any god damned back up? Is he fucking stupid? I swear when I find his sorry ass I'm going to beat it black and blue." She went on in this fashion for several minutes before she finally wore her anger to a dull roar. She still grumbled and growled, but tried to remain calm.

When her torrent of cussing ended, Serenity looked out the window just in time to see a black blur run past them. She looked at Jas and smiled "They won't be alone for long. And I think you'll have some competition for kicking their asses, cause Jack just ran ahead of us." In response, Jas put her boot to the petal and stomped it down, saying "Sorry Jack, but I'm kicking my man's ass before you."

After a few minutes of running, aided by the wind. Jack made it to the beach. When he arrived at the burnt land, he started scanning the beach for their scent. Within moments he caught the scent of freshly oiled metal and pine. One name ran through his head: *"Mikey."* He started off down the trail, but he caught another scent, one that was unfamiliar to him. Tilting his head up, he sniffed the air, tasting the smell. What he caught nearly made him empty his stomach: Brimstone, sulfur, death and misery stung his nose. He could feel himself pale as he contemplated the meaning of the scent, then he shook his head, steeled himself, and started again.

Taking off down the trail, he ran into the hills from the beach. His feet pounded the ground and he pushed himself down the trail. Every few strides of his run, he would mark a tree or a bush or draw a symbol in the dirt. He had intended to leave a trail so they could find their way home again. His breath came in great gasps as he ran, wondering to himself *"How far did they go into this place? I feel like I've been running for hours."* He stopped at a fork in the trail, and sat upon a stump to catch his breath. While he caught his breath, he examined his surroundings with a mixture of tension and curiosity. All around him, the forest seemed different: The trees felt dead and hollow, despite the summer season. Leaves were wilted and dry, and all throughout the forest, an uneasy silence filled the air. No birdsong was heard, nor the sound of insects; no squirrels danced in the trees or deer in the hills. It disturbed Jack to his core as he began to realize the power that they were facing. When he could go no further, he sat upon a stump and tried to communicate with the forest.

Meanwhile back at the beach, Serenity and Jasmine were scanning the beach for any sign of the boys. Serenity was the first to pick up the trail, finding Jack's shoe print in the mud by the trail's head. She hollered out for Jas, who came to her side and stared off down the trail. Just as Serenity started down, Jas put a hand on her shoulder and said "Wait, we need to be smart about this. We can't just go charging down the trail with absolutely no idea what's on the other side." As Serenity opened her mouth to protest, Jas shushed her and continued. "What happens if the boys come back and we're out roaming the trail? We'll be constantly separated from each other. We need to hold this point and wait for them. Besides, Jack gave us an order to follow the lead we got this morning." Sighing her resignation, Serenity nodded and replied "You're right. So what should we do?"

"Well, we could either wait here for them to return, or we could go back to the hotel and work on the herbs.

Serenity thought for a moment and said "We wait here. If Jack isn't back in an hour, we're going in after him." Jasmine nodded and lifted a stick from the ground. She walked to the muddy entrance to the trail and planted it in the dirt, a marking that they're waiting if the boys don't see them right away. Then they turned and walked back toward the truck, to wait for the rest.

Meanwhile, further on down the trail, Mike and Jeff pressed on, despite the growing thickness and closeness of the foliage. Pushing aside or breaking the overgrown branches and bushes, they pushed deeper down the trail. Mike huffed out a breath and said "It looks like the trail gets thicker as we move on. Maybe we should stop and wait for the others."

Jeff shook his head. "We need to find where this goes. If we're lucky, it could lead to the damn thing's hiding spot." Jeff swore as he cut a sapling down out of his way. Sighing, Mike muttered a short prayer as they continued onward. After a few more minutes of pushing, slashing and breaking, they finally cleared the brush. Jeff gasped as he laid eyes on the structure before them. In the small valley, surrounded by brush, sat an old, dilapidated building. It looked to be a small, single story cabin, built of stone and iron. Mike whistled softly and whispered "That reminds me more of a bunker than anything. Why would someone have a bunker all the way out here?"

"I've got no idea bro." Jeff shook his head as he held his axe a little tighter. His eyes darted back and forth as he spoke "The tracks end here. So either it took off, or we found its den." Mike growled as a strange, tortured scream came from the building.

Jack jumped to his feet as a scream echoed through the forest. He tore off down the left side of the trail calling out "Mikey! Jeff! Where are you guys?" His calls were met with silence so he kept running. He transformed into his wolf form and starting bounding through the brush. He leapt over fallen logs and dashed through the brush as he sped, following Mike's scent. Finally, he came to the clearing, just next to Mike. He transformed back and ran up to them. "Mikey, goddess damn it what the hell happened?!"

Mike turned to Jack and said "I don't know. We found this footprint and we followed the trail to this," he waved his hand, gesturing at the structure as he continued, "place. We were only here for a couple minutes when this horrid, blood curdling scream rang out." Jack turned toward it, looking it over. It looked like a small fallout that people would've built in the cold war: The foundation was solid concrete, with few wooden accents. The windows had thick bars on the outside, and the door was solid steel. As he looked it over, the cabin seemed to emit a strange, glowing mist from around the foundation. He readied his staff as he said to Mike and Jeff, "Toss your bombs through the window bars. Let's see what we're up against." Nodding, they took the purification bombs out of their pockets. In unison, they crept toward the windows on either side of the door that faced them. Just as they pulled the pins, the cabin screamed again. It shrieked at such a high pitch that the brothers had to drop the bombs and put their hands over their ears in a desperate attempt to block out the sound. As the mist began creeping from the canisters, Mike and Jeff attempted to kick them at the foundation wall that surrounded the bottom of the house, before they retreated back to Jack.

Once they got a certain distance from the cabin, the shrieking stopped. The bombs went off, engulfing the house in a pure white smoke. Jack started muttering a binding spell when a cackling laugh was heard in the forest behind them. The trio whirled around to come in close contact with a pale, twisted face and shiny black horns. Two fangs hung down from the upper gums, which were exposed because of the creatures twisted, demented smile. Out of instinct, Jack struck the creature with the top of his staff, letting forth a burst of lightning to stun the creature. It howled in shock and pain as it backed off, rubbing his eyes and staggering from the power. Mike slammed into the creature's stomach and chest with the head of his hammer, and Jeff took advantage by swinging around to decapitate the demon.

Suddenly, the demon's hand whipped up and he laughed, catching Jeff's axe, which caused it to stop in mid swing. A ball of dark energy collected around its fist as he slammed into Jeff's exposed stomach. The wind rushed out of Jeff's lungs as he went sailing through the air, only to crash a few feet back past his brother, toward the house. The sight of his brother laying on the ground, gasping for air enraged Mike, who turned toward the demon. He clenched his fists and spat through grinding teeth "You'll pay for that you sorry son of a bitch! I will CRUSH you!"

He hefted his hammer and charged, howling in rage. When he was close enough, he brought his hammer down with his full strength. The creature laughed and dodged the hammer blow, kicking Mike in the back and the head as it did so. Jack cast a ball of pure light energy, which with the flick of a wrist, the demon sent careening into a nearby tree, causing the energy to dissipate. As the demon rushed him, Jack held his ground. He drew his shoulders back and switched his grip on his staff, letting loose a flurry of strikes while channeling magic into the wood. Shocked, the demon tried to retreat from the onslaught of blows, to which Jack responded by advancing, driving him back to the tree line.

No matter how many strikes Jack could lay down, the creature seemed to keep dodging and deflecting them. Jack upped the speed of his attacks and tried switching styles, but the creature side stepped the line of attacks and brought its talon's through Jack's left bicep. Jack gnashed his teeth together as his nerves burned around the wound. He looked at that twisted, demented grin and he could feel the Spirit rising. With one fluid, powerful motion, Jack encased his right hand in a ball of pure lightening and brought it around, striking the creature in the side of the head.

Stunned, the creature withdrew its talons and stumbled backwards, right into a crushing blow to the side from Mike's hammer. As the creature went flying, Jack slammed the staff into the ground and shouted toward the sky. The other two leapt to his side as a whirlwind kicked up, sweeping them up above the tree tops and carried them away from the battle. A tide of grasping, wheezing laughter followed them as they retreated from the site.

Once they were back at the beach, Jack set them down. He doubled over and started breathing hard, holding his left arm and using magic to bind and seal the wound. He gnashed his teeth and let out small groans as the flesh and muscle mended. Around him, the brothers did the same, trying to recover from their pains. They groaned and moaned and rubbed their shoulders and ribs. Aching from the fight, they limped to the side of the road, where

Jasmine and Serenity were waiting with the truck. Jumping out, Serenity ran over and embraced Jack with enough force to stagger him. As he recovered his balance, he returned the hug with his right arm, keeping the left at his side.

While they embraced, Jas walked up to Mikey and she asked "What the hell happened out there? We picked up on enough power to break a small mountain."

Mike rubbed the back of his neck, but before he could respond, Jeff chimed up "Things went to hell, that's what happened." He doubled over as his ribs started to heal. Mike looked at Jas and nodded, saying "That's about it. We followed the trail, tracking the demon. When the trail ended, we were at this old looking hunting cabin. Bout the time we got there, the place let loose this horrible screeching sound. That's about when Jack found us, and we went to purify the place."

Jeff chimed in again, interrupting his brother, "Then, out of nowhere, this freaky ass looking thing snuck up behind us and that's when shit got fun. We fought the damned thing off, but it gave almost as good as it got. Eventually, Jack flew us out of there."

Jack and Serenity looked at him as Jack said "Be realistic, if we had stuck around, it may have kicked our asses." He looked at Serenity and said "This thing is stronger than anything we've gone up against before. We may need to call up some help for this."

Serenity shook her head "No, we need them to watch maps and make sure nothing else comes up. Besides, if we leave Troy undefended, we'll run the risk of something moving into our energy cash."

Exhausted, Jack collapsed on a stump and put his head in his hands, saying "We don't have many options Serenity. That thing has some serious power."

He cast a look back at the trail, feeling a sense of unease. He continued "Alright, well it's a bit past lunch, so let's grab dinner and gather our wits." Looking at Serenity, he said "We'll need stronger purifiers. The ones we've got now barely did anything."

After a few moments of resting and healing their wounds, Jeff looked to the sky. He stared at the sun for a few minutes, then he smiled and said "It is in between 3:00-4:00"

Jasmine pulled out her phone and said "You're close, it's like 4:05."

Jack's shoulders slumped slightly as he sighed and said "Well, it's too late to get lunch. What does everyone want for dinner?"

After a few moments of discussion, the group settled on going to the local cracker barrel for a nice, home cooked meal. The group piled into the car and Jack readjusted the seat, grimacing "Serenity, next time it's just you two, you're driving."

Jas snapped back "Why the hell can't I drive?"

"Because you're only five foot something and you fuck with my seat every time you do."

The tips of her ears went red as Jas sat back in the back seat, huffing as she folded her arms. The rest of the car ride was quiet.

Chapter Five: Family Business

By the time the family arrived, their moods had perked up from the gloomy places they were at. They walked into the nice restaurant and saw that it was close to empty. Only a couple of old people and a family occupied the dining area. A quick word from Jack got the group a corner table in the far back corner. Isolated from the few patrons that they shared the building with, the group split up. Jack held his chin resting in the palm of his hand, nursing a glass of raspberry lemonade. Mike and Jeff were playing checkers by the fire. Jas was cruising the gift shop, looking for a souvenir, and Serenity was studying the menu, looking for her dinner. Finally, Serenity said "I love you." She looked at Jack, who smiled and kissed her cheek softly, before he returned to his pose. Sighing, she continued,

"Honey, you need to relax a bit. Stressing about this creature isn't going to make him go away."

"It might. Maybe if I think really hard he'll just vanish." Jack smiled at the old joke, which brought a smile to Serenity's face as she replied, "There's the smile I love to see."

She kissed him as Jas scooted her chair out and plopped down into it. After a moment, she beamed and pulled out a stuffed wolf. With a quick spell, she brought it to animation, making it dance around the table and wag its tail. The three began to laugh at the little creature's antics as it began to run at Mike, who felt the creature pulling at his pant leg, attempting to drag him to the table. The brother's finished up their game and walked back over. Taking the seats on either side of Jasmine, Mike and Jeff came back to the table and sat down. When the group was all back, the doll returned to its nonanimated state. Jas picked it up off the table, and Jack signaled the waitress. When she came, they all placed their orders, and when they were done she said "The chef's got his work cut out for him tonight." She winked at Jeff and turned around slowly to walk away. Jeff eyed her up and shrugged, then turned to Jack and asked "So, what's the game plan big guy? When do we take this thing out?"

"I've got no clue what this thing even is, bro. As for taking it down, I don't know where to begin." He looked at Serenity and asked, "Do you think the boy is involved in any way, or is he a bystander?"

Serenity replied "I don't know. As all records go, he and his brother were the first people to be actually attacked. It seems like, before them, it was just the land that was under attack. Maybe the kids were just an accident?"

Mike cracked his knuckles and mumbled, "The last accident that fucker will ever make."

Jas patted her man's shoulder and said "Whatever the case, I don't think that this thing is as powerful as it seems. It got the drop on you three. Maybe it's just a coward?"

Jeff rubbed his side and said "No, I can confirm its strength. " He winced as he continued "It's powerful and it packs a hell of a punch when it gets the chance."

Jack shook his head and said "I still think we need to call in the rest of the family. In reality we're fighting a two fronted war." He held up one finger. "First off, we've got this mystery demon that has some serious power. It obviously knows the wooded areas and loves ambushing us." A second finger joined the first, "Second is the nature itself. We have to heal it for the townspeople and for our own benefit. If we leave this blight on the land, it could spread and we'd lose a lot of power as it went along. We need help."

Serenity spoke up "If we pull the rest of the family, then we're pulling the people who are watching over Troy. We'd be leaving our own borders unprotected, abandoning our oath to the mayor, and let's not forget that Leon's got school. We can't just pull him out."

Jas nodded her agreement "Yeah, she's gotta point. It's Leon's last year and he has enough on his plate as is. Let him have some time to just patrol and get a grip on his stuff."

Jeff snorted "I dropped out and..."

Mike interrupted his brother by slapping him upside the head, then he said "Just because you dropped out and got by doesn't mean it'll happen for everyone. Need I remind you that Jack nearly killed you when he learned that you dropped out?"

Jeff rubbed his head and went quiet.

Serenity looked at the group and said "No one is dropping out of school. Leon stays home. Period. If need be, I guess we can call James in, but we promised the mayor we would always have a garrison in the house. We don't need something moving into the town under our nose and making a mess of the place."

Jeff snapped back "Who the hell cares? We can always return to Troy and fix the land. We need to help these people"

The argument went on for a while in this fashion. Nothing broke it up until the waitress returned to the table, bearing two big trays that were piled high with piping hot food. As she passed them around and set them in front of the group, each member dug into their plates. Mike and Jeff attacked their chicken platters with great ferocity, as chunks of chicken and bits of potatoes and carrots scattered the table. Jasmine, Serenity, and Jack ate in a more civil manor as they put their napkins in their laps and used the silverware within them. As they ate, few words were spoken, beyond the grunting and gestures for salt and pepper.

A clattering of forks on plates and collective sighs rang around the table. They nursed their drinks as the waitress came back and took their empty plates from in front of them. Eyes met, but no one wanted to say what was on their minds, for fear of a new argument breaking out.

Finally, Jasmine spoke up by saying, "Look, it's obvious that we're not going to reach an agreement tonight, so I say that we go back the hotel and wait for sunrise. Once the sun's up, then we can all go to this cabin and assess the situation. If all five of us can't take this thing on, then we call for backup or we retreat." After a moment's thought, they all nodded and muttered their agreement. Jack stood up and said "Alright, I'll get the check, you guys go on out to the truck. I'll catch up." They rose, pushed in their chairs, and started walking out; only Serenity held back. When the others were gone, she walked up to Jack and wrapped her arms around him, whispering, "I love you honey." She squeezed him tightly, kissing the back of his neck before she walked away. He smiled and watched her leave. When she was around the corner, into the sales room, he picked up the bill and wandered over to the register. Putting the check down on the counter, he took out his wallet and pulled out his debit card.

The woman's smile was ear to ear as she said cheerily "Did ya'll enjoy your meal?"

"It was delicious, thank you." Jack replied absently as he felt a sensation prickle up on the back of his neck. He cast a quick glance around as the woman rung up the bill. Taking the receipt she offered, he smiled to her and wished her a goodnight.

As Jack walked to the truck, a cold wind suddenly picked up. Looking around, he saw the truck was running. Walking toward it, he staggered and stopped, his vision fading. Falling to his knees, the last thing he heard was Serenity shrieking "JACK!" before he collapsed to the ground.

Serenity bolted out of the truck and ran over to his prone form. She shook him in a frantic state, saying "Jack! Jack please wake up!" The others joined her, looking at Jacks unresponsive body.

Mikael looked up toward the cracker barrel and snarled "Somebody will answer for this."

Jasmine put a hand on his shoulder to hold him back. When he turned to face her, she pointed to Jack's body and said to the group "Look."

They all looked on in astonishment as a golden thread wrapped itself around Jack's body. Jasmine continued "I think someone wanted to see him. That's the mark and color of the gods."

Serenity pursed her lips in thought, then said "Jeff, Mike, get him into the truck. If we stand out here too long someone will be bound to notice this" She gestured to Jack's body as she spoke, then she continued "Jeff, you drive us back to the hotel. Once we get there, mike's going to have to put a shadow on Jack and carry him up to the room."

Jeff and Mike wordlessly picked him up and Serenity jumped in the back seat of the truck. They laid Jacks head in her lap and Jasmine rested his feet on hers. Jeff then got in the driver's seat and set up his mirrors. Mike shut Jasmine's door and took his place in the passenger seat. When they were all in position, Jeff started up the car and pulled away.

Jack sat up with everything around his smudged and cold. The dark air rushed around him like a vortex, but only produced a muffled sound. Looking around, he got to his feet and tried to summon his magic. His efforts were met with a feeling of disconnection and emptiness. He swallowed, fear rising in his chest as he fought against the strange influence. As he fought, the air around him shimmered a rainbow of colors, each one the opposite of the energy that he tried to summon. When he noticed this, he stopped, realizing that the very air in this strange place fought his efforts. He looked around, then noticed one area of the void was darker than the rest: The air was thick and black, and not even the sound of the air came from the dark door.

A voice flowed from the dark space. "Don't worry my boy, you're completely safe." He focused on the space and saw a figure emerging from the shadow. The tall, muscular, pale skinned figure rolled his shoulders and golden wings appeared from over his shoulders. His pearly white smile shown from behind his ruby red lips as he said "I'm here to offer you some help." He motioned with his right hand and the air rushed to the space in between them. The air condensed and swirled faster, making a whirlwind. When it finally died down, a table, with two chairs on either side of it, appeared in the space. Sitting in the chair closed to him, he gestured to the other chair and said "Please, sit my friend."

Hesitation mixed with the fear in Jack's heart as he sat crossed from the stranger. He attempted to put on a tough front. He sank into the chair as he said "Who are you? Why am I here?" The man's smooth, gilded laughter fell from his mouth as said "This is what I find so amusing about your kind: You like to act tough when you're faced with something you don't understand, yet I can feel your fear." Jack leaned back, shocked by his words. As he tried to regain his composure, the mysterious man started laughing again. Finally, enraged by the man's laughing, Jack snapped, "What the fuck do you want from me?!" The laughter ceased as suddenly as it had started, the amber eyes of the man went dark with rage and disrespect. In a low, deadly serious tone, he spoke slowly "Do not pretend to threaten

me young man. I am far older and more powerful
than you know." Jack went silent, repressing his
anger.

Meanwhile, the group pulled up at the hotel.
Jeff pulled up to one of the side doors and shut the
engine off. He and Mike then got out of the car, with
Jeff going to the doorway to make sure everything
was clear and Mike going around to Serenity's seat.
Serenity opened her door and lifted Jack's still
unconscious head and neck up. Mike slipped his
arms between her and Jack. He hooked Jack's
underarms and slowly, Mike pulled him off of Jas
and Serenity. When his feet were off of her, Jasmine
slipped out the door and went around to help Mike
support Jack's lower back.

Little by little, they got Jack out of the truck.
Serenity slipped out of the truck and asked Mike
"Will you be alright carrying him Mikey?"

Mike chuckled in his deep, hearty way "I've carried him before." He hefted Jack up and laid him across his shoulders in a fireman's carry, "I can do it again." He mouthed a quick spell and Jack's form shimmered, then disappeared.

When they were ready, Jeff opened the door and led the way as they silently walked to the elevator doors.

Oblivious to Jack's anger, the figure sighed and said "Look, in laymen's terms, I'm here to help you. You can take it or not, but your pack is going to be in trouble."

Jack tilted his head and asked, "What do you mean? Do you know something about what's going on here?"

The mysterious stranger waved his hand at the air. At his motion, a portion of the air solidified and expanded, until it represented a flat, glossy, black mirror. With a flick of his wrist, he produced a scene on the mirror. The black mirror took the form of the old cabin in the woods, only it was fixed up and busy. The trees around it were lush and vibrate, deer filled fields around it, and the land itself seemed vibrate and happy. Jack could see figures going in and out of the cabin: Men clade in leathery armor, with bows laid across their backs. A woman stood in the window, she wore fine robes of black and silver. From his angle, Jack could see her holding a book in one hand and a glass in the other. He looked back to the figure and said "This was a House."

The figure nodded, replying "Yes, but we did not build it. You see, it was found by a small team of scouts that I sent to examine a strange aura that was attracting creatures to the house."

As Jack nodded, the figure continued "As early as six months ago, that cabin was the home of a group of my finest scouts, and one of my wife's favored enchantresses. They were my sons, and she was her daughter. Three months ago, they discovered a crypt beneath the cabin. After a few days of trying, they managed to breach the seal, only to discover what lay within was a terrible monstrosity. Within an hour, my sons were slaughtered, the land poisoned, and the enchantress was driven away. We found her three days later, lying in a ditch. Her wounds were too severe to treat on her own. We all failed in our duties: My wife and I failed to foresee and protect our people, and our warriors failed to slay this monstrosity. Now your pack has to help us clean up our mess."

Jack's face paled and he asked "Wait. If your warriors were beaten by this creature, then how can we beat it?"

"You need you clear your mind, and relax. I can help you, but you must listen."

Suddenly, the mist shimmered and distorted itself. When the image returned, it was an elaborate bedroom. The walls were made from polished obsidian rock. The floor was covered in a soft looking, deep red carpet. In the center of the room sat a large, four poster bed made of a deep cherry wood. Silver lace was elegantly hung between the columns. The bed itself was graced with silver pillows, and comforter, and a tall, dark haired woman laid upon it. The silver blanket covered a portion of her body. She must have failed to notice Jack, because she beckoned to the mysterious stranger with one finger as a soft, sensual voice *called out, "Erebus, darling, come back to me. I miss you terribly." Jack's eyes widened as he breathed out, "Lady Nyx." Recognition bloomed on his face as he looked back at the smiling man as he whispered "Soon my love, soon" The woman smiled and blew a kiss to him, then the image faded.*

Erebus looked back to Jack and smiled, saying "My beautiful wife beckons. I better get home to her and let you go to yours. Just remember, when the time comes, look to the shadows. He smiled as Jack bowed his head, awestruck by the whirlwind of power and events that flowed around him. Erebus looked at him and said "Remember my words, and awaken."

Gasping, Jack opened his eyes and shot up. He instantly regretted it as the blood rushed to his head and made his vision blurry and his head spin. He rested his head in his hands and groaned softly, waiting for the sensation to stop. When it did, he looked around and tried to gauge his surroundings. It didn't take long before he recognized the feelings of his wards and the Serenities scent that lingered in the bed. He heard the soft mummer of voices through the wall. Moving himself to the edge of the bed, he knocked on the wall three times.

The voices picked up, and Serenity slowly peeked into the room. Seeing Jack sitting on the bed's edge, she rushed into the room and hugged him. As she held him, the rest of the group followed in. Jack held up his hand to stop the torrent of questions that flowed toward him, and he said "I have no idea what happened to me. All I remember is walking out of Cracker Barrel and blacking out. Then I was in a really weird place, surrounded by black mist and a vortex. Then, Erebus walked out, made a table appear and he told me some history about the demons hide out."

Serenity's eyes went wide as she said "Lord Erebus? Are you sure? What did he look like?"

"He was pale, with long black hair, amber eyes, and golden wings."

Jasmine held up a hand and looked at him in disbelief. "Golden wings?"

Serenity bowed her head and whispered "It was him then." She then looked to Jasmine and said "You were right, the gods did want to see him."

Jack nodded his head, trying to gauge how long he was out. He looked at the night sky, the moon was high and full. He sighed and turned back to the group, saying "All I know is, I think we have some help against this thing now." He got up and looked at the pack. Their faces held a variety of emotions: Serenity's held a mixture of worry and relief, Mike was tired, Jasmine looked suspicious and careful, and Jeff looked happy for the news. Jack smiled slightly and said "Get some shut eye. Tomorrow we're going hunting again, and this time we're going to end this fucker."

Jasmine, Mike and Jeff looked back as they walked back into their room. Jack drug his hand crossed his face, groaning as he did so. Serenity draped her arms around his shoulders, nuzzling them and whispering, "My poor baby." She kissed his neck softly before she started rubbing his shoulders. As she massaged him, she said "I was so worried about you. When I saw you fall I had no idea what had happened."

Jack said nothing, but he rested his right hand on hers. He held his hand there for a bit, then he took it away to rub his eyes. As he pulled his hand from his face, he asked "How long was I out?"

"About two hours."

Jack nodded and then he said "I don't think I'll find sleep tonight my love." He turned his head to face her, and was met by the sparkle of her beautiful hazel eyes. A smile crept across his face as he kissed her over his shoulder. She smiled, then she got up and said "I'm going to go to the bathroom honey."

As she walked away, Jack sat up and walked over to the window. He looked out over the highway and sighed in exhaustion. He sat in the chair as he reflected on what Erebus had showed him, the moon falling over his face. Knowing he wouldn't find sleep, he rose from the chair and walked over to where his duffel bag lay by the dresser. He unzipped the side compartment and pulled out a shiny, black leather tome, emblazed with the image of a red wolf's paw. As he walked back to the chair, he opened the book of power and began reading. He became so engrossed in his reading that he barely noticed as Serenity walked out of the bathroom and laid down on the bed.

She lay there, on her side with her head propped up by on hand, while the other stroked the area next to her. Looking at him sweetly, she whispered "Baby, come to bed please. It's cold and I need you to help me warm it." Jack looked at his fiancé and he sighed "Honey, please. For once, I'm not in the mood." He smiled at the weird sentence that came out of his mouth. Yet, once he looked at her, he saw that she was fully clothed. She looked at him and said "No I'm serious, this bed is really cold and I want to cuddle you. I can't sleep without you."

Jack put his book down on the nightstand and got into bed with her. As he snuggled under the covers next to her, he said "You know I may not be able to sleep right? I was just unconscious." He laughed and she joined in, her lighthearted laughter lifted Jack's spirits as he said "I love you." She smiled and soon she drifted off to sleep. Her deep, even breathing accompanied him as he stared at the ceiling, trying to get lost in its hypnotizing patterns. When he couldn't take lying still anymore, he gently slipped out from under her arm, and walked to the door. On his way, he gingerly grabbed his boots from their place by the door. Holding them in one hand, he reached the other toward the door. As he opened it as slowly as he could, he kept looking back over his shoulder, making sure he wasn't waking her. Once he had it open enough, he slipped out as quietly as his trained body would allow. Closing the door softly, he walked down the hall, toward the small alcove that held the elevators. He slipped in his feet into the boots as he waited for the elevator to ride up. While he waited, he laced them tight and put the hem of his sweatpants over the laces, keeping them tucked into his pants. As he stood and pressed the door to the elevator, a voice spoke over his shoulder: "Long night brother?"

He turned around and he saw Mike standing directly behind him. He sighed and nodded, saying "Yeah, you could say that. I just" he shrugged his shoulder "couldn't sleep." Mike nodded and said "Yeah, I know. I couldn't sleep either." He looked back to his room and he sighed, then asked "Jack, can I ask you something?"

"Sure big guy, what's wrong?" They paused as the elevator dinged and the doors opened. Jack and Mike stepped into the elevator and pressed the ground floor. As the door closed "Look, after you and Serenity announced your engagement, it made me think. I want," He looked down and bit his lip, then he said, "I want to propose to Jas."

Stunned by the news, Jack was speechless. Then he said "I didn't think you guys were that serious. I thought you and her were against marriage?"

Mike shook his head and said "We're not against it, we just didn't know if the time was right. But we were talking about it tonight and, well, we are starting to change. We want to be together forever." They were silent for a moment, as the floor display ticked over, each number lower than the last.

Finally, as the elevator neared the ground floor; Jack broke out in a huge grin and he slapped Mikey on the back, saying "Well good for you big guy, I'm happy for you!"

The elevator opened and they stepped out, and crossed the lobby into the night air. As they walked around the building, Jack felt something nagging in the back of his mind. Drawing a deep breath, Jack sighed and said "I have a bad feeling Mike. Stuff is going downhill and we've barely got any ground left. I just hope that we can end this thing quickly and go home."

Mike just looked off into the night sky, his face set in a grim expression "I smell a storm coming." Jack nodded and looked toward the moon. After a few moments of standing in place, Mike patted Jack on the back and said "You'll lead us through big guy. You always have before." Jack smiled and nodded at his best friend, suddenly thankful for the company. He watched as Mike turned and walked back into the hotel, then he strode out behind it, enjoying a brisk night air. Once he reached the edge of the lot, he undid his boots and removed his socks. Stuffing the socks inside, he picked up his boots and walked out onto the field of grass behind the hotel. He adventured out for a bit, looking for a spot with a clear view of the horizon. When he finally found a small area that wasn't obstructed by buildings or light posts, he rotated until he faced east, then he sat. He closed his eyes and began to meditate on the day. His energy melded with the earth and air around him as he sat upon the grass. He focused his breathing, making it a steady, even keel that melded with the breeze. As his own energy melded with the world around him, he felt the calming steadiness of the world, which brought him a sense of peace.

When the sun began to crest over the treetops, he felt a presence approach him. He opened his eyes, and was greeted by a pat on his shoulder. He turned to see Serenity, wrapped in a blanket, standing over him and looking concerned. She sat next to him and said "You weren't in bed when I woke up. I was worried until Mike let me know you were out here. Is everything alright honey?"

He met the worry in her eyes and smiled softly "Everything's alright baby. I just," he turned and met the sun's watch as it rose through the morning sky, "I needed to walk, to clear my head." She sat next to him and put her head on his shoulder, then whispered "It'll be ok." Draping his arm crossed her shoulders, he nodded softly. He pulled her close as they watched the sunrise together.

Chapter Six: A Plan Revealed

Jack and Serenity walked back into the hotel lobby to find the pack gathered around the same table as they were the previous morning. Sitting down, Jack looked around and waved his hand, motioning for them to move in. Once they were all within whispering distance, Jack said "We need to end this thing. If we don't, then we're putting a lot of people in harm's way."

They were quiet for a moment, then Jeff spoke up. "How do you plan to do that? I'm all for marching in, kicking down the door, and going bare knuckle against this thing. But, the last time we tried that, we got our asses kicked with very little to show for it."

Mike nodded his agreement, but Serenity said "That's true, but we didn't go in as a pack. If we go in like we trained to do, and fight like real wolves, then it won't have a chance."

"Alright Alphas, what's the plan?" Mike had leaned in close, eagerness in his voice. He clenched one hand closed, resting the fist on the table.

Serenity got up to get her and Jack some food and Jack some coffee as he outlined the plan "Mike, you and Jeff with go into Lycan form, stalk around either flank of the cabin and lie in wait. Once it answers my challenge, wait until it gets clear of the cabin's porch and ambush it. When you two have it tangled, I'll transform and join in. That should provide sufficient distraction for Jas and Serenity to sneak in, set the smoke charges and cleanse the house. Once its energy source is cleared, we can remove this thing safely." They sat in silence, mulling the plan over.

She returned with two plates, piled high with eggs and bacon, fruit, muffins, and biscuits and gravy. She set one plate in front of Jack and the other at her spot, sat down and dug in. As she ate, Mike said "This is risky. What if he overpowers you or he has something in the cabin that is set to go off when they go in? There is still a lot we don't know." Jeff shook his head, agreeing with his brother, but Jasmine said, "We don't have much of a choice. If we wait, this thing will keep killing the land and destroying the energy until it leaves a dark void that is absent of life. We have to stop it now, or we'll be facing a much larger foe in the end."

"And what if it kills us? Did you think of that?" Jeff started to get louder, so Mike whispered harshly "Speak up, Jeffy I think there are some people in the next town over that didn't hear you clearly." Jeff looked at his brother, who continued "We have no idea who may be involved with it, if any of them are. You keep talking loud, then it's going to know our plan." Jeff took a deep, shuttering breath and said "All I'm saying is that this could be a suicide mission."

Mike turned and faced him fully, saying "When isn't every day of our lives a suicide mission? Why wasn't charging down that trail a suicide mission? Brother look at what we do for a living. We LIVE in a suicide mission."

Jeff sighed, admitting defeat. Mike turned back to Jack and said "I say we go at twilight, that way we have the peak hours of our strengths. Plus, it'll be easier for us to sneak into the woods and launch the ambush." Jack nodded his agreement, then he yawned, saying "I'm going to try and get some shut eye before the attack. Jeff, you and Mike take watch. Jas, you go gather the remaining supplies and Serenity will start brewing the purity smoke so we can go to war. Wake me up about three so I can start preparing. At dusk, we attack." The group nodded and a sudden air of calm enveloped the table.

Chapter Seven: War-torn

They finished the meal in silence, a storm of emotions rolled through the table. Apprehension, Fear, Determination, all mixed together as they glanced at one another and wondered the same thing; would they triumph over this. No one spoke a word, not wanting to speak the unspoken fears. They knew that it was dangerous, but they didn't have much of a choice. They walked back to their rooms, still in silence. They stopped outside their doors, and Jack made the first move. He kissed Serenity, then looked back at the group and said "Remember, wake me up at three."

As he walked into his room, Mike and Jeff were debating on how they should split the watch. "I'll take the first watch. That way you could get some sleep, Mike."

Mike shook his head "Nah, I'm fine. Besides, you could use the break. I heard you tossing and turning last night. It seems like you didn't get much sleep either."

"I'll be fine." Jeff said as he cracked his fist. Finally Jasmine spoke up "How about this: One comes with Serenity and I while we shop, the other remains here. When we return, the one who stayed with Jack can go out if we need any more items, and the one that went with us can watch the rooms." Both boys nodded their heads, and Jasmine pulled out a quarter. She set it on her thumb, then gestured at Jeff "Ok Jeffy, call it."

"Heads."

Jasmine flipped the coin and they watched as it hit the floor. "Tails." She said, then she looked at Mike and asked "What are you doing."

Mike looked at the door, then the girls and said "I'll go with you guys."

The debate settled, they went into Jasmine's room to ready themselves. Mike put his hammer in the form of a cane, Jas's whip went around her waist, and Serenity's dagger was made into a pendant, which was worn around her neck. Mike offered Jeff his forearm, which Jeff took and shook. Then Jas, Serenity, and Mike left the room for the elevator, and Jeff settled into his bed to watch TV.

The walk to the store felt like a death march. The sky was darkening with sickly green clouds, and there wasn't any sound coming through the air: No cars on the street, no people talking on the phone or birds singing. People who did walk, walked with their heads down and away from the small group. Mike leaned in to Jasmine and whispered, "You'd find more cheer in a funeral. What's with everyone?"

Jas shuddered and moved closer to him "I don't know, but it's giving me the creeps." They looked around and eventually found the small store. As they entered, they were stopped by a group of townsfolk. The group stood a few feet from the pack, who stood with the door at their backs. The hair on the back of Mike's neck stood on its end. He walked in front of the girls and said "Why, isn't this ominous. May I ask what this is about?" His hand went down to the point where the handle of his cane met the shaft. His grip tightened on the spot as the other group pressed closer. The man at the group's head pointed at pack and said in an eerily empty voice, "We told you to turn back. We warned you to leave. Now you will suffer."

Within a few seconds, the zombie-like mob changed. Their mouth's dropped open, and they started shrieking. The pack cringed at the sound, which resembled nails sliding down a chalkboard.

They continued at these inhuman pitches and their mouths stretched far wider than they should. As they shrieked and yelled, some fell to the ground, twisting and contorting their bodies in a terrifying manner; the remaining few charged the group, only to be met with Mike's hammer as it extended from the trick cane. Serenity drew her dagger and shouted "Ambush!" Jas turned to see another group of possessed people blocking their escape. She yelled, "Run! We have to get inside." With a mighty stroke of his hammer, Mike bowled over the first group and growled "Let's move!" He led the way as they ran into the store, the possessed ones right on their heels. Some were running, others were crawling, but all were chasing the pack.

Meanwhile, back at the hotel, Jeff was watching daytime TV when he saw the sky darken. He rose from the bed and walked over to the window. As the clouds pressed closer to the town, he swallowed and retrieved his axe from where it lay by the his bed in his room. By the door sat two small black duffel bags. He grabbed them both and went into Jack's room, sealing the entrance with a glyph. It was then, that he heard a noise coming from the hallway.

Curiosity overwhelmed safety as he went to the door to try and see what was going on. The hair on the back of his neck began to rise as the energy fields around the rooms began picking up the threat. He softly opened the door and peered outside. He was met with the sight of all the doors on the floor slowly opening, and people shuffling out. Their eyes were glazed and their steps hollow. No words were spoken as they marched in this fashion. Unnerved by the display, Jeff shut the door and locked it, then he armed the defenses and readied his axe. Mumbling under his breath, he said "I seriously doubt we have until dusk." As he finished his sentence, he heard an inhuman screech from the hallway. The heat in the building rose as the fire fields kicked up, a wall of flame blocking the doors in both rooms.

The smell of burning flesh and hair assailed Jeff's nose, takin him back to that night: *A moonless night found sleepy Troy terrorized by a maniac. He and the pack stood in a derelict library, facing down a giant of a man with jet black hair and scars crossing his skin. The fires in the braziers burned the remains of failed experiments and pieces of humans. Jack's yelling and throwing magic around as the rest of the pack try to fend off the horrid creatures. Jeff buries his axe in one's head and back hand's another, sending it sprawling on the ground.*

Suddenly, a low growl fills the room, followed by the sadistic, cackling laugh of the butchering monster. A deep, gravelly voice rings out "Alrighty heroes, let's see how you handle this lil doggie. With a wild swing of the blood stained butcher knife that occupied his fist, he slashed through a thick black rope, and a piece of the wall fell. Behind it stood a huge black hellhound, with eyes as red as fresh blood and fur as black as its master's hair. It howls, then fades away.

Jeff shakes his head and comes back to reality. He looks around to see the walls shaking, and the fire starting up at the other door. A fresh wave of the smell assaults his nose as he says "Fuck me, I'll never get used to that shit." He heard a thump at the window behind him. Turning around, he was met with a smiling teenager. The gleaming white teeth would have been impressive if the mouth baring them hadn't been contorted and twisted into a demonic grin. The teenager started thumping against the wall in an attempt to break the glass.

The sudden commotion of noise woke Jack up from his nap. Looking over to Jeff, he yelled "What the fuck is going on?"

"A zombie mob." Jeff chuckled, then set his face into a serious look and continued "Seriously though this shit is fucked up."

He jumped from the bed as the thing broke the glass, raining it down on where he just lay. Jeff jumped in front of him and with one fluid strike, he removed the head from its shoulders. As the blood dripped from his axe, a thumping noise was heard at the door, and Jeff said, "Yes we are under attack. I don't think the fire is holding them at bay very well, cause they're still trying to break it down." Swearing violently, Jack grabbed his bag and said "Give me some time." Rushing into the bathroom, he donned his armor and gear: black cargo shorts that hung past his knees, a black tank top with a leather back, his spiked armband, his belt that contained a hidden short sword, and his combat boots. As he opened the door, he saw Jeff standing at the window, his axe was buried in the wall and his body grappling with two smaller kids. Jeff threw one out the window and pinned the other too the wall with a pocket knife. Jack rushed out and drew his sword.

As Jeff removed his axe from the wall, Jack grabbed his staff and planted it in the carpet, summoning forth the magic from the wood. From the next room, he heard the cracking and splitting of wood. Looking around, he saw that Jeff grabbed the supplies from their room while he slept. He breathed a sigh of relief as he heard the door finally give way. Snarling, he barked out a spell that engulfed that adjoining doorway in fire, searing any who would dare cross it.

Back at the store, Mike, Jas, and Serenity stood in the stock room, surrounded by pallets of fruit and cans. They used magic to maneuver the crates into blockades, forcing the townspeople into three lanes. Each member stood in one lane, fighting off the possessed people.

Serenity said "Try not to kill them. We need to stay…" Her words were cut off as a person came over the barricade and hit her over the head with a watermelon. Her fury breaking loose, she tore the thing's throat out with her nails. Wiping the blood on her pant leg, she turned to Mike and Jas and said "That's it, no mercy." Mike grinned a savage grin and howled. Turning toward the possessed people, he drove forward. His hammer flashing and people going down under his assault. Finally, the last one fell under his attack.

Just as he set his hammer on the ground, they heard a thunderous explosion rip through the air. The group immediately went out the loading doors, and searched for the source. Turning, they saw a column of thick, black smoke rising from their hotel. Serenity immediately took off running, putting as much speed and energy into her muscles as they could take. She poured every ounce of energy she had left into her legs, and when that was depleted, she drew from the air around her. Soon, she became a streak of light. When she arrived back, she saw that the hotel had become a blackened shell, burned out and smoking from a recent explosion. Trembling, she fell to her knees and began to wail. Mike and Jas came behind her shortly after, and Mike went silent. Hands trembling, he walked over the rubble. Collapsing beside Serenity, he bowed his head and sobbed softly. As they wept, the sound of shifting rock and debris moved through the air. Racing to his feet, Mike dove into the wreckage. He moved chucks of rubble and flung them into the air, digging to keep his hope alive of finding them.

After a few minutes of frantic digging, he found the shattered remnants of Jeff's axe among the rubble. He held the shattered weapon across in his hands, dumbstruck. Looking around, his eyes fell upon the bent remains of Jack's sword. His mouth feel agape as he knelt in place. Unable to hold them back anymore, his tears fell into the ash, forming little wet clumps of dirt. He started muttering to himself "Please, please brother be there. Brother, you can't be dead." His tears began streaming down his face as he sobbed, "Jeff, Jack, you guys can't be dead. You can't!" He roared out, striking a broken bit of a wall, leaving a massive indent in the stone. He fell to his knees and put his head in his hands, his crying echoed into the wind.

Seeing him break, Serenity realized that their fear had been confirmed. She bowed her head and felt the tears form in her eyes. Jas walked over to Mike, leaving her alone at the edge of the ruins. As she cried, her own spirit became enraged. She was pissed. Pissed at this demon for taking her fiancé, pissed at them for dying, pissed at herself for not being there to stop it. Two white balls of pure power formed at her fists as they clenched. She slowly rose to her feet, head still bowed. Holding that pose, she turned toward the beach and the cabin in the hills. In a flash of red light, she took off running toward the hills with one thing on her mind. This single thought slipped into the air as she spoke, her voice low and deadly "I am coming to kill you, you fucking bitch."

Chapter Eight: Dead and Separated.

Jack and Jeff woke up in an endless void. They stood in a blackened patch of ground, surrounded by a never-ending stretch of flat land: There was no mountains, no hills or streams, no breeze. Around them, the world was a shade of grey. It was a lifeless void, empty of all feeling. Jack spoke one word: "Dead." He couldn't believe it. He was dead. His mind ripped back to his unknowing final stand.

He had summoned up his wall of fire, holding their small room against the possessed townspeople. As they threw themselves against the door, he had no idea that they had thrown a small tank of propane into the room until he saw the silver flash and heard the explosion rip him apart.

He fell to his knees and hurled. When his stomach was empty, he cried. Jeff walked over and sat next to Jack, silently resting his hand on his brother's shoulder.

They sat like that for a few moments, before Jeff heard the unmistakable sound of footsteps softly approaching them. Whirling around and ready to fight, he stood face to face with a small, fragile looking man. The man walked with his hands folded and his back bowed, a worn brown hood hiding his face. He raised his head and looked at the two boys before him, sighing. When he met their eyes, tears of starlight shown in his eyes as he said softly "I'm sorry boys. I don't want to do this, but I have no choice." Jeff was about to snarl back when Jack rose to his feet. He sighed and said, "I understand Death." Turning to face the small man, he rested a hand on his shoulder, saying, "I don't blame you." Despite the situation, he allowed a small smile to play across his face "It's good to see you again, Myth 'Aral." Jack bowed his head, trying to show respect to the old man.

Death smiled back "I was hoping I would see you as an old man, who had lived his days well and came to me with honor, as Jota did." The tears slipped down his face as he continued "Yet now I must take you as a young man." His breathing shuttered as he attempted to compose himself. When he had regained his composure, he said "I've been instructed to take you both to the judges. They will decide what will be done with you."

Jack looked at Jeff and said "We don't have much of a choice brother. I guess it's time to meet our fate." When Death wasn't looking, Jack winked at him and said "Let's go bro." Jeff's shoulders rolled back, showing determination and strength as he walked along side Jack, Death lead them through the grey land.

Soon, they left the plain grey landscape them behind, and the emerged into a field of long, uncut grass. A huge volcano erupted in the distance that filled the air with tortured screams and moans. In front of them stood three golden statues in a marble courtyard. Jack marveled at the grand, marble pillars that ringed the courtyard. In between the pillars, a gate of wrought iron, gold, and lead bars closed the circle.

A huge line of people stood outside a pair for wrought iron gates that led into the court. Death took Jack and Jeff to a side section of wall that dissipated as they got closer. The discontented chorus of the dead grew louder and angrier as they saw the two boys cross into the courtyard ahead of them. Death stopped at the missing section and said "Jack, you must proceed first and you must go alone. Jeff, you will wait here." Jeff looked at Jack and offered his hand to Jack. Jack looked at the pro offered hand and grasped his forearm. Pulling him forward, they embraced in a warrior's hug. They stood there for a moment before Jack pulled away, squared his shoulders and marched into the courtyard. Looking back, he saw the fence move back into place behind him.

As he walked, he took note of the positions: The largest of the beings sat in the center of the ring of marble and stone, before a slightly elevated dais. The smaller two sat on either side. Upon closer look, Jack was surprised to see veins of pure energy running all through the statues. He knew at once who they were: The three judges of heart, mind, and soul. They who laid judgment upon the dead and decided their fate. An involuntary shudder racked his being, causing him to stop mid stride. The magnitude of their power washed over him, making him feel small. He shook it off and proceeded to the dais.

As he approached the center, the statues seemed to shimmer and move, as if they were alive. When he came to the center point, he ascended the steps, and knelt at the center. He held that position in silence for what seemed like ever, finally the center judge spoke "Jackson Franklin Williams, born June 25 of the year 1994, Wolfish warrior and grey Mage. You have been brought before this council for judgment of your life. Do you have anything to say before we render our judgment?" Jack looked back at Jeff, who stood beside Death with a stonefaced, yet determined expression set into his face. In that instance, all he could think about was his family: Serenity, Mikey, Jasmine, James and Leon. He sighed, then decided. His face locked into one of strength, he looked at the judges and said "Honorable spirits of the fallen. I am a simple man who lived a simple live trying to help other people. I ask that you send me back to my wife and my pack, so I may complete my task." The judges sat in silence at first, but then the walls around them started to morph.

They melded together to form a grey wall, similar to the one used by Erebus when he met with Jack outside of Cracker barrel. Upon the wall, pictures that showed all of Jack's life, from his birth up to his death. It revealed how he discovered his power at a young age,

Jack was laying in the hospital bed, under restraint and guard. His step mother bursting in the room and attempting to strangle Jack while he lay defenseless. The brutal power that surged into his being, breaking the restraints and lifting that woman off the ground by her throat, his teeth sharpening, his arms bulging with muscles that weren't there before. His grandfather, resting a hand on Jack's shoulder and abating the rage that stormed through him.

Then the pictures shifted, and it showed him gathering his pack and saving his hometown from a ravenous necromancer. *The pack stood at the doors of a decrepit library, evil energy pouring from it. A group of young people, scared and unsure, against a force of evil that had taken and ruined many lives. Jack turning and facing his people, seeing the fear in their eyes. Then he turned and raised his hand, and willed his power forth into a ball of white light. With a battle cry, he sent it spiraling forth, into the wall of darkness. Then it flashed to the end: The pack, bloodied and bruised, but standing around the corpse of the fiend that had killed so many people. In one instance, they raised their voices in triumph as it sank it: It was dead and they had won.*

Once more, the picture faded and changed. It showed the moment he proposed to Serenity in Colorado. *Jack was standing on a balcony, overlooking the rocky mountains of Colorado. He held the small, black box in his hands as fear and uncertainty pierced his heart. Taking a deep breath, he turned and faced Serenity, who was standing behind him expectantly, waiting to see why he called her outside. The tears glistened in her eyes as he knelt down and asked her. Then the smiles as she said yes.*

Tears filled Jack's eyes as he saw all the battle and conflict in his life. His head was turned down when the judges spoke again "We have all reviewed your life, Jackson. You lived one of honor and dignity. You were a warrior, a protector, a lover, and a brother. You have been chosen to go to paradise and live your days in comfort."

Jack was stunned, but he soon found fury as he spoke "How can you sentence me to that?! I need to go back to my mate and my family! I refuse to go to paradise! You need to send me back!"

His protests fell on deaf ears, because the judges returned to their golden form and didn't hear his words. He joined with Vulcan, and howled in rage as he sent a barrage of energy at the statues, demanding they answer him. His wrath was stopped as two guards formed from the mist, and he was drug back toward death. When they dropped him off by Death again, he had tears streaming down his face. Jeff rested a hand on Jack's shoulder, causing him to rise and embrace Jeff. Tears ran down his face onto Jeff's shoulder, who wordlessly stood there. After a few moments of the embrace, the guards returned and laid their hands on Jeff, who saw it was his turn and walked in without looking back.

Jack watched Jeff's judgment with horror. He knew that Jeff was never a perfect man, but he saw all the things that he never knew. It went in the same form of Jacks, starting with his youth. *Jeff was standing there, in a rundown kitchen, eyes turned toward the ground, as he was being yelled at by his father. When he refused to meet his gaze, his father struck Jeff in the face with a beer can and stormed out the door. Once he was gone, Jeff let a single tear fall, before going to his room. The scene flashed forward again, a couple years into the future. His father was yelling and screaming again, but this time, when he went to strike Jeff, his hand was stopped. Jeff's eyes turned a fiery red as his fist smashed into his dad's face. He kept striking until his dad laid on the ground, cowering with his arms above his head to try and abate the fury of blows that rained down. Once he was done, Jeff grabbed his coat and stormed out.*

Again the picture changed, it showed Jeff in a nearby park. He sat on a bench, opening and closing his hands. He kept working on summoning fire and heat. A figure walked up and sat down next to him, and offered Jeff a small bag of green. Jeff took it and started to walk away. When the figure got up to stop him, Jeff turned on the man and began to beat him the same way he beat his dad. The blows kept smashing into the man's face and body: Ribs were broken, along with his nose and cheek bones. Jeff collapsed his lung and brought him to the ground. The dealer cowered on the ground, but Jeff stood over him, starring at his victim. He slowly raised his hand and brought the fire to his palm. The dealer's eyes went white, and Jeff unleashed a torrent of fire on him. He walked away, leaving the smoldering corpse on the sidewalk.

Jack stood there in shook as he watched the pictures changed again and again, each detailing more violent acts of aggression: Jeff robbing a bank, the demonic binding, the murder. Jack remembered seeing somethings in the news but he never knew that Jeff was responsible.

The judges' verdict was handed down without hesitation. "Jeffery Scott, for your unending abuse and disgrace to your life, to your pack, and to your power, we damn you into the fiery mountain. You will spend your days in agony and pain, in repentance for your crimes." Jeff didn't cry, or whine, or whimper. He met the center judge's eye and nodded in silence. Turning on his heel, he held his head high, and walked away from the judges without another word.

When they were back with Death, Jack looked at his best friend stunned. "Jeff... Why?"

"I don't know." He wouldn't meet his eyes.

Death looked at them both and said "I'm sorry to rush this along but, who is going first."

Without hesitation, Jeff said "I'll let the angels of torment take me." He looked at Jack and smiled "Don't cry for me brother. I won't break."

Jack's eyes filled again as two dark robed figures landed next to Jeff and bound his hands behind his back. They then put a hand on either of his shoulders and lifted him. His parting words were "You can break my bones, but you'll never break my spirit!"

Jack bowed his head and let his tears fall to the dusty fields. Seeing what Jeff was, it filled him with a strange sense of respect. He was a bastard, yet when he took the oath to fight, he fought just as hard to keep the peace. Jack looked towards the angels, flying away with his friend, taking him to the mountain of fire and death. He started to wonder what the demon side of Jeff would do.

Death rested a hand on his shoulder, interrupting Jacks thoughts. He nodded to the old spirit, and turned away from the sight. Allowing death to guide him, he began walking away. Away from the Judge's circle, away from the line of dead souls, and toward the golden gates of Paradise.

Later that night, Jack was lying on a soft, downy comforter, surrounded by bookshelves that towered over his bed. In the next room, sat a 70" flat screen TV, Xbox one, and all the games he could ever desire. The bathroom was a cavernous room with marble counter tops and a black and white checkered tile floor. The shower was made to resemble a cave, with the water cascading down around the cliffs. Every meal was delivered to his door, and if he wanted to, he could use the phone next to his bed and special order food at any time.

He had everything he wanted, yet sadness rested in his heart. He rose from the bed and went to the large bay window that sat across from it. He looked out beyond the gated paradise, over the plains of those in limbo, and to the mountain of fire. Resting a hand on the window frame, he shook his head noiselessly, unable to shake the thoughts of his battle brother in torment

"Jeff should be here. He may have been a bastard in his early years, but he died a warrior's

death. It's not right" Once more, tears found his eyes as he thought.

A familiar voice coughed behind him, causing him to jump from his thoughts and turn around, which brought him to be face to face with Erebus. Anger quickly replaced the sadness as he met the god's eyes.

Snarling, Jack grumbled "Some help you turned out to be. My pack's going to be slaughtered, my best friend is in the mountain of fire, and I'm stuck in this thrice blasted paradise!" He threw his hands into the air and screamed at the god "WHY!? Why did you let this happen to us?! You said you needed us, you said we needed to stop that damned demon! Look where we are now?!" He balled his fist and got within a hairsbreadth of Erebus "If I hadn't pledged to your service, I would break your immortal jaw for this." Anger seethed through his veins as he turned his back to the god and stared out the window, fuming.

Erebus stood silently for a few moments, allowing Jack to cool down. When he judged it was time, he simply said "Let's go."

Jack didn't even look over his shoulder "Go?! I'm going nowhere with you!"

"Do you want to save your family or not?" Erebus crossed his arms impatiently "We can do just that, but you have to both trust me and hurry." Jack turned around, his anger slowly being replaced by curiosity. When he said nothing, Erebus replied "This is not how my wife or I wanted this to go, but like it or not, we're here. Now, if you're able to let go of your anger toward me, we need to go."

Without complaint or question, Jack followed him out into the streets of paradise All the small houses looked identical: Neutral colored siding, nicely manicured front lawns, some spirits even planted native trees and plants of their home. A samurai meditated under a cherry tree, which always seemed to be blooming, an old woman tended to a rose bush, which had beautiful red and white flowers on it.

All around the houses though, were beings in white armor. They walked through the streets, quietly observing the paradise. They each had wings of silver or white, and wore the same armor: A sleek steel breast plate, arm guards of silver, and steel pants. A slender short sword hung at all the belts, and some had bows and quivers across their backs. Each face was obscured by a white hood, leaving nothing to light. The bowed before Erebus as they passed, and opened the gates as they approached.

Once they were clear of the gates and prying ears, Erebus said "Remember the path out, because you'll need it when it's time."

"Time for what?" Jack was puzzled, but he followed the god as they walked through the tall grass. Jack took a second to examine his surroundings and was shocked. There was nothing: No hills, no trees, no houses or buildings of any kind. The spirits just wandered around, moving through the grass without a sound. He looked back and saw that the gleaming golden gates where now wrapped with steel plates. Jack shuddered, and he figured out why they were called the Grey Plains: No color, no sound, no comfort or pain. It was all grey.

He returned to Erebus, who had stopped at the base of the mountain. Jack looked up at the imposing black gates and swore he could hear the screams of every damned soul within. The scent of brimstone and sulfur filled the air around the gate. Standing on either side were two imposing guards, each clad in dark iron armor and wielding large poleaxes. They bowed their heads before the god, and Erebus waved them away. When they were gone, Erebus looked back at Jack and said "When it's time for you to get back to the surface and fight."

Jack was shocked as he met Erebus's eyes. Erebus smiled, and said "That's right son, you're breaking out of Death."

Chapter Nine: Darkness and Fire

As they stood outside the gates, Jeff was dropped off inside of the prison. His carriers shoved him too his knees and wrapped two heavy, burning chains around his forearms. He looked at the veiled angels and sneered "What? Is that all you've got? You fucking panzi assed bastards can't do any worse than he did."

He spat at their feet, which earned him getting kicked over as a heavy leather boot slammed into his breast bone. As he laid there, struggling to regain his breath, one the angels replied calmly and without emotion

"Keep quite you disgraceful display of mortal flesh."

Jeff rolled to his feet and leapt at the angel, only to be stopped mid-air as a cold hand caught the back of his shirt. He was turned around, to be faced with a giant demon, clad in iron. Jeff hung their as his face was caught in a stream of foul, rotten air that emerged from the creatures mouth. A voice resonated from the deep, black iron helmet as the tormentor spoke "Jeffery Scott, welcome to hell."

The tormentor then removed a large, curved knife from his belt. He held Jeff in the air by his neck and sliced open his shirt. As the fabric fell to the ground, the heat of the room ignited it, leaving a pile of ash to lay on the ground. When he sheathed the blade, the tormentor slammed Jeff's exposed back against an iron cross. Jeff's skin bubbled and hissed as it burned against the white hot metal. A yelp of pain escaped his lips, which caused the tormentor to laugh. A deep, booming laugh that reverberated off the walls.

With one hand, he held Jeff against the cross as he used the other hand to tie Jeff's hands to the cross beam with heavy leather binds. When Jeff was sufficiently secured, the tormentor stepped back. It was then Jeff saw the fire pit, and sticking out of the metal rim were iron handles. Jeff snarled and tried with all his might to break free, but try as he might, he couldn't break the binds that held him. The tormentor laughed again as he watched, then he said "Try as you might, pup, you'll never escape your retribution." Laughing again, he walked over to the fire pit and selected a brand from the fire. Holding it close to Jeff's face, he said with a sickening tone of glee "Now the fun begins."

Chapter Ten: A Dark cloud.

Jasmine and Mike raced to catch up to Serenity as she charged toward the demon's lair. Air whipped into their faces as they struggled to catch the furious Serenity. As the trio burst onto the beach, they finally closed the gap and caught up to her. Jasmine lunged out and tackled her. They rolled onto the sand, as Jasmine struggled to hold back Serenities force. All the while, Jas was yelling "Serenity! Stop! This won't bring them back. Charging off to your death isn't going to solve anything."

Serenity stopped her fighting long enough to look into her eyes. When the fury abated, she broke into tears of fury and misery as she cried32 "He needs to die. He stole Jack from me, from us." She sobbed as she said "He needs to die. He needs to die!" She howled one last time, then collapsed into a broken, sobbing mass in Jasmine's arms. Jasmine held her close and she rocked Serenity gently, stroking her hair and saying nothing. Mike walked up slowly, he hugged both of them and joined his tears with hers.

After a few moments of sitting together in the sand, Serenity ran a hand over her face, wiping away the tears. Between sobs, she said "We need to call for reinforcements. I know I said not to, but we're out gunned, outnumbered and we need the extra fire power."

Jasmine nodded "We'll find somewhere to hole up and make the call."

Mike cleared his throat "Then we'd better move." Pointing off into the distance, they saw a party of townspeople shuffling toward the beach. Serenity and Jasmine rose from the sand. The group moved toward a small hill, where they each laid flat and observed the group. As they watched the shambling group, they sky around them darkened and condensed in a greenish mist. A scent of sulfur and brimstone assaulted the groups noses so strong, it forced them to turn their heads.

When they looked back, the sight took their breath away. The once human beings were different: Their skin was a brittle grey, and sunk in over their bones. Their bodies shambled and jerked in awkward motions. Their eyes were replaced by hollow black pits. Worse still, emblazoned on their skin were glyphs marking their demonic master.

Serenity looked at them in horror. She muttered to herself "Husks." Turning to Jasmine, she said "We can't go back to the hotel, so where should hole up?"

Mike looked around and he said "I do remember a small campground just to the east of town, down the other side of the beach and into the forrest. If we can get there, we may be able to find a camper or a tent or something to take shelter."

Nodding, Serenity replied "Alright, let's get moving."

As they slunk away, the cloud spread. It fanned out and engulfed the town in its dark, misty haze. Serenity could feel the earth cry out for help as the energy was changed and hurt. The poisonous cloud scoured every building and every human, leaving nothing good standing. The group moved slow and low, trying to avoid detection. However, once they reached the road, the original group of husks saw them. A terrifying screech was heard as they drove toward the pack. Mike rose to full height and willed his hammer to his hand, just as Serenity pulled her bow from the void. Jasmine summoned a shield around them as Mike held the front. In an instant, the small pack was surrounded.

After a pitched battle, the pack managed to slaughter the husks. When they had the fight won, they made haste to the forest. They wove from tree to tree, using a combination of magic and skill to keep their speed constant. Once, they broke into a small campsite. Panting and nervous, the group looked around for a suitable shelter. The only thing they could find was a decent sized five person tent that had been abandoned. Serenity looked at Mike and said "Break it down as best you can and let's move it. We need more cover than this." She looked at Jasmine and continued "We'll get the firewood and whatever supplies we can carry." Nodding their agreement, they set to work. In short order, they had scoured the campsite. Though they found little, what they did find was good enough: A cooler of prepackaged food and trail mix, a first aid kit, a separate cooler with alcohol, a fire axe, and some magazines, a cell phone, and four duffle bags of clothes. The tent was broken down and the medical supplies, trail mix, and medical supplies rolled inside. They left behind the alcohol, phone, clothes, and magazines. Mike hefted the makeshift bundle onto his shoulders, looked at Serenity and asked "Where should we go? We need a place with good cover and safe."

Thinking quickly, Serenity looked around and said "We need to get into the more wooded area of the camp ground. We can use what's left of the energy and cast a protective shield to hide us from prying eyes." Mike looked at the fire axe that was leaned against the tree. Scooping it up, he carried it with his free hand. Before Serenity could ask why, she heard him mumble "When we find this demon, I'm going to burry this axe in his skull for you, little brother." She turned her head to hide her tears, as she led them deeper into the campground. As she walked, she muttered "I love you Jack." Turning her head toward the sky, a single tear dropped from her face as she said softly "Happy anniversary."

Chapter Ten: Hell's breaking loose.

Jack sat up in his house, absently minded watching TV. In his head, he kept playing the event over and over again in his head, wondering how they would get out. The scene of Jeff's torment played in his mind:

He had followed Erebus across the Grey Fields, and into the fiery prison. He stuck close as Erebus weaved through the pressingly dark, incredibly hot halls. When he reached a certain door, he turned to Jack and whispered "Mark this symbol" he pointed to the glyph above the door, emblazed in red "for this is Jeff's cell." Erebus pulled a key from his pants pocket and clicked the lock. As the door opened, it was immediately blocked by a hulking figure. The body was cloaked in black leather and chains, and his face was obscured by an iron helm. A quick word from Erebus and a flash of silver was all that was needed for the tormentor to leave the room. When Jack looked into the room, he was horrified.

He saw his friend, strapped to a red hot iron cross, shirtless and bare. His body covered with scars and burns, his hands held in place by iron bars that dug and burned into his skin. His feet bound by iron chains. Yet, despite the obvious pain and torture they inflected on him, his eyes shown with that same determination, that same fire. When he saw Jack, he smiled and said, a hint of sarcasm colored his voice "Well, here I was thinking that I was going to spend eternity with just me, and these limp dicked tortures. It's good to see ya buddy."

Jack couldn't help but smile at the words as he replied "It's good to see you too bro."

"So, what are ya doing here? They want you to see what happens to degenerates like me?" Jeff snorted and spat, the saliva bubbled as it hit the air.

Erebus looked mildly astonished at his bravado and he said "Actually, I'm here to get you boys back to the surface. You and Jack are needed to help undo what's done." At a wave of his hand, the smoke in the room joined and hardened into a black screen. When the wall was ready, Erebus conjured up an image of the above ground world. Jack and Jeff gasped together as they witnessed their pack in a pitched battle on a road, followed by the pack running through the forest. Jack waved his hand, sending the image away and said "Alright, let's get back already."

Erebus held up his hand "Not yet. First we need to break this one out, and I have to re-forge the equipment that you lost in your death."

Jeff looked at him and said "Well, how long is that going to be? I mean, not that I'm in a hurry to get away from this agonizing pain or anything." Jack rolled his eyes as Erebus replied "Only should take about a day or two. The trick will be getting you out of here, Jeffery."

Jeff did a little shrug and said "Alright, I can last."

Jack looked at Erebus and said "How will we do this?"

The plan was this: Erebus would have two of his soldiers take the place of the tortures that would take over Jeff's punishment. Another would drop off Jack's staff and armor. Once he had his gear, he would walk out of paradise by himself. He would have to cross the Grey Fields and find his way into the mountain by memory. Once inside, the fighting would begin as he would have to free Jeff from the cross and heal him. Then, they would have to race to the night bridge, where Erebus and Lady Nyx would lay claim to their souls. Once they were in the Shadow halls, they would simply be returned to the surface.

A simple plan, yet so much could go wrong. Jack's forehead began to bead with sweat as the time drew closer and closer. He thought back to his fiancé and chuckled humorlessly.

"Four years." The trip was supposed to be an anniversary trip for them, and a vacation for the pack. "Four years and now…" Tears began to fall as he reminisced on his life, and deep in his gut, the familiar fear grew again. He feared that they would fail, and Jeff and he would forever be stuck here until their pack fell.

He hurriedly wiped away his tears as his door knocked. When he opened it, two men dressed in gleaming white armor stood on his doorstep. They carried it inside and set it on the floor of his foyer. Before they departed, they bowed in unison, saying "A present from the Lord Erebus, sir." Jack thanked the men, and closed the door when they walked away. He stood there, admiring the solid oak chest. It was a simple thing, made of darkened oak wood, with iron hinges and handles.

Finally, his eagerness overwhelmed him. Jack unlatched the locks and opened the lid, seeing what Erebus had delivered. His jaw dropped as he pulled out a staff made of solid oak, and engraved with runes. The body was stained a deep, rich amber hue, that accentuated the runes and designs that were inlaid in cool steal. The crown of the staff was adorned by a pentagram, wrapped in the triple moon crest. His clothing had been woven from blackened leather and soft cloth, like it was never broken. Excited, he changed from his heavenly robe and donned his clothing, enjoying the weight and feel of this new gear.

His excitement quickly faded as he looked out his front window. From there, he saw the fiery mountain, just as dark and foreboding from within the safety of his house as it was standing at the base of the mountain. He drew a shuddering breath and said to himself "I guess it's time." He hardened his heart as he grabbed his new staff and ventured out the door. Walking down the street, he cast his gaze around, and found it very different. The samurai spirit was dressed in full armor, with a hand resting on the grip of his katana. His gaze, too, rested on the mountain. Around the other houses, the spirits were dark and nervous, each casting looks around the gates and at the guards. What bothered him the most was the lack of noise, as the only sound to be heard was his staff clicking the ground. Jack quickened his steps to the gates. As he approached, the guards raised their arms and stopped him.

"Where are you going Jackson?" The guard looked suspiciously at his new attire and continued "No one is allowed out of Paradise at this time. The damned ones are stirring up trouble in the mountain and no one is allowed…" The guard never got to complete his statement, as a fiery rock crashed into the fields. Acting quickly, Jack slammed his staff into the ground and used a force of air to knock them back. With the guard distracted, and the gate rocked open, Jack bolted through the opening. The marbled street gave way to a tightly packed dirt trail as he made his way into the Grey Plains. Blades of grass bent and weaved as he ran, the force of the wind carrying him with such speed that the angelic enforcers couldn't keep pace.

As he was running toward the mountain, his thoughts raced. *"Did Jeff not wait? Did he do this? Is this a part of the plan?"* He forced himself to shake off his thoughts and redoubled his energy, running as fast as he could to the mountain.

When he arrived at the black gate, he was greeted by the screeching and howling of angels in pain. He peered around the splintered gate, into the courtyard. Within that courtyard, it was nothing short of complete chaos. Jeff was free, his remade axe in his hands, and unleashing his fury on his tormentors.

Jack moved into the gate and sent a wave of wind towards Jeff's group, knocking them off their feet and breaking up the fight. When Jeff rose back to his feet, Jack called out "We need to move, Jeff! Let's go!" Jeff turned with astonishment toward the gate. When he saw Jack, he smiled and yelled back "Right behind you." He hook half a step, then turned and buried his axe into a tormentor's chest.

When he wretched his axe free, he sprinted toward the gate. As he came up to where he stood, Jack turned and started to run, falling into stride with Jeff. They took off, leaving the guards to deal with the damned souls that they had spent an eternity torturing.

The very landscape blurred around them as they charged though the fields of the damned souls.

Neither man minded the tears streaming down their face as the wind stung their eyes, nor the hands of the damned tried to stop their break for freedom. Behind them, fire flew from the mountain as chaos reigned in prison. Several times Jack had to send a ball of wind toward an angel or Jeff had to knock them aside with the head of his axe.

Yet, for all the effort of the spirits, each man driven by a force stronger than the binds of hell. All Jack could see was Serenity's smiling face, all he heard was her voice, beaconing him onward. All Jeff saw was that demon. The horrible laughter rang in his head, causing him to run faster, snarling and growling. All he could think was *"I will have my payback. I'm coming for you, fucker."*

After what seemed like an eternity, they reached the bridge of shadow. Erebus and Nyx stood waiting, a company of guards and servants waited with them. As Jeff and Jack crossed the bridge, the servants cleared a space around them, closing them off from the mob of spirits that chased them. As they stood within that circle, each servant transferred a slight amount of energy into the two, healing their exhaustion soothing their muscles. Meanwhile, the forces of hell amassed at the other end of the bridge. The mob twisted writhed, a chaotic mass of howls and screams. A large angle in black stepped forward from the group and yelled "We demand that your return those souls. They are the property of Hell and must be returned to us!"

Nyx yelled back "My husband and I had claim to them long before they died. If anything, you stole our souls!"

Erebus smiled at his wife, then he returned his attention to the mob that sat on his doorstep. He placed a hand on the pommel of his longsword, and strode leisurely up to the angel who spoke at the mob's head. When he was but a hairsbreadth from the being, he stopped, and loudly proclaimed "No matter what you may think, they have crossed into our realm. They belong to us now, so leave before you start a war." His eyes narrowed, and he drew his blade a fraction from its sheath.

The group dispersed rather quickly, no one wanting to risk open combat with Erebus. The last one to leave was the dark angel, who locked his eyes with Erebus, but eventually backed down and turned away, walking with his head held high. When they were all gone, he spat at the ground and returned across the bridge. When he stood before the two boys, he stopped and smiled, saying "Well, that went rather well boys."

Jack nodded, then looked at Jeff and asked "What the fuck happened?! You broke out way to early bro."

Jeff shrugged and gave a wicked smile in reply, saying nothing. Nyx rolled her eyes and said "Alright, let's get you two back to the surface."

Chapter Eleven:

Reinforcements

"What the fuck happened here?! How can you guys be gone for five days and manage to fuck up an entire town?" asked Leon.

Serenity regarded the newest member of their pack with exhaustion. They had been hiding out for two days, waiting for the rest of the pack to join them at their makeshift camp. James looked at them and said "I'm with Le here, this is seriously wrong."

Serenity sighed and responded "Look, we don't exactly know what happened. This all started with this demon just randomly attacking us. Then the whole town turning on us. I've got no idea what's going on here, so just calm down and help us."

They were all grouped around a small table than straddled the fire pit. Laid out across the table were sheets of notebook paper: One with a rudimentary map of the area, with the town and surrounding forest sketched out. Another held rough estimations of the population and how many were out right dead and how many were turned into the husks. Leon threw his hands up and shouted "CALM DOWN! You want me to calm down?! Jack and Jeff are dead, we're in the middle of the forest, with demonic creatures running around, and you tell us to calm down?"

Serenity walked over to him and threw a powerful upper cut that landed square on his chin, knocked him on his ass. Snarling in frustration and exhaustion, she growled "Jack was my fiancé, Jeff was one of this family. I grieve for them just as you do, but we still have a duty to the rest of the world to strike this fucker down and save what people we can. Now pick your ass up off the ground and actually be fucking useful!" She turned on her heel and stormed into the tent.

As she sealed the flap behind her, James asked Jasmine "Ok, so what is the situation as of this moment?"

"Right now, we're ok on food and necessities. We've got shelter and defense. As of now, our biggest weakness is knowledge. We need to go gather intelligence on the town and figure out how to stop this madness before it consumes the world."

Mike stood at the edge of the camp, leaned on his hammer and stared off through the trees, keeping watch. Silent until now, he spoke "I'll take Leon and scout the town. We'll also try and grab some supplies to keep the camp up. Jas, honey, maybe you should go talk to Serenity, get her calmed down again. James can take up my watch."

Leon settled the katana crossed his back and said "Yeah Jas, tell her I'm sorry. It was just shocking to find out Jack and Jeff were gone. I'm sorry." He hung his head as he apologized. Jas ignored him, and crossed the camp to Mike and kissed him softly, whispering "Come back to me baby."

Mike placed her hand on his chest, just over his heart and replied "I'll always come back, my sweet." With that, he and Leon turned and headed off into the town.

The two strode out of the camp, into the sickly woods, toward the town. Leon asked Mike "So what happens now? Will you and Jasmine lead or will Serenity lead by herself?"

Mike waved the question away and replied "Now isn't the time for those questions. We'll answer them when we make safe the area."

Leon shrugged his shoulders and turned his attention to the woods around them, growing ever sicker at the sight. The trees, once green and vibrant were now sick and brown. The leaves littering the ground were brown and sticky, clinging to their pants as they walked. Leon kept scanning the forest, straining to sense for other life. After a few moments of nothing, he whispered to Mike "Is everything in this forest dead? Did nothing survive?"

Mike replied in a sober tone "It is most likely, young one. Creatures like this rarely leave anything alive or untainted. It is more likely that anything that survived has fled the area by now."

Leon shuddered at the thought, but said nothing. Instead, he returned his focus to their surroundings.

As they walked, a clearing came into view. Seeing it, the two dropped into low crouches and carefully crept to the break. Mike took cover behind a fallen oak, while Leon scurried into a bramble of bushes. From their spots, they could make out a small group of husks wandering around an old campsite. Leon winced at their visage. Their grey, taunt skin looked at like old canvas stretched too tight across the frame. Their eyes were sunken and hollow, and their movements were like a puppets that strings were being jerked all around. Mike growled ever so slightly, and raised his hammer in preparation. Seeing his friend's action, Leon drew his blade ever so slightly. In unison, they leapt from their hiding spots and rushed the camp.

Before the husks could react, Mike crushed the biggest one's head, and Leon had impaled the one nearest him. It wasn't long, however, that the husks responded. One jumped onto mikes back, clawing his face and biting at his neck. Leon saw this, but before he could intervene, the remaining two tackled him and forced him to the ground. They struggled like this for a few minutes, Mike trying to pry the husk from his back, and Leon kicking and trying to regain his feet. Finally, Mike was able to reach his hand around and grab the back of the husks neck. With a mighty throw, he pried the thing free and flung it into a tent. As the fabric ripped and collapsed under the impact, he ran over to Leon, and swung his hammer. As the blow connected, Leon was able to free himself. He scrambled to his feet and took his stance. Within short order, they hand managed to cut down the last of them.

As their corpses lay in the dirt, Leon sheathed his blade, then proceeded check Mike's neck and back for serious injury. Finding none, he whistled softly and said "Damn dude, you must be made of chainmail or something."

Mike laughed and replied "Stone and steel Le, stone and steel." The skirmish done, they proceeded toward the town.

When they reached the town borders, they sprinted toward the closest house they could see. When they reached the yard, they dropped into low crouches and crept along the edge of the buildings. As they reached the corner of house, Leon peered around and gasped. In the streets, there were dozens of husks, just milling around aimlessly. Wandering from house to house, down the street, or just standing in place, they all seemed to be just awaiting direction from their master. Leon went back around the wall and shook his head. Sensing his thoughts, Mike whispered "There is a lot of them over there." He didn't mean it as a question.

"Noo not at all. It's all clear, there's even a group of satyrs and pixies dancing on rainbows. Of course there is, you big dope." Leon replied sarcastically. He shook his head and looked back around, he continued "I don't think we'll be able to make it past all this undetected. We may have to…"

He was stopped in mid-sentence when the ground began to rumble. Suddenly, a violent eruption shook the ground. The sound of concrete and metal bursting filled the air, along with the husks howling. The two watched as the horde started to rush further into the town. When the coast was clear, they slowly and carefully ventured out into the driveway. They sat silently behind a van, and waited for the quaking to stop. When they finally subsided, Leon asked "What do you think that was?"

Mike readied his hammer and said "I don't know, but we should probably find out." With that, he snuck past Leon into the street, following the tail end of the horde. Leon whispered under his breath "Goddess guide us." He drew his sword and followed Mike down the road.

Their progress was slow, as they tried to avoid areas where the demons were thickest. As they got closer to the center of town, they made even less progress, as they navigated the maze of business buildings and apartment complexes. They rounded a corner, and nearly ran headlong into a cluster of husks. Thinking quickly, Leon turned and dove into an abandoned house that sat just off the center of town. They crept up the stairs, into a bedroom. From the windows, they could look out over the central park. As they peered over, they saw a sight that left them in shock.

In the center of the park, in the mouth of a gaping crater, stood Jack and Jeff. They wore new versions of their old armor, with remade staff and axe. All around them were piece of stone and metal, and a throng of husks trying to claw them to pieces. Jeff stood just before Jack, planted atop a mound of rubble, axe swinging through the air. All around him lay dead husks, most missing limbs, but all cleaved open and bleeding. Jack was throwing spheres of lightening all through the horde, shocking them and leaving them immobile and weak. A fierce smile played across his face as he took to the melee and started using his staff to smash into them and deflect their attacks. Jack moved through the horde, climbed the mound and stood beside Jeff. Growing tired of the fray, Jack slammed his staff on the ground, sending a rippling shock wave around them, fling the husks back in all directions.

All the while, Leon and Mike sat there, dumbstruck that their fallen comrades had returned. Leon's excitement soon overcame his awe as he stood up and yelled at them "Jack! Jeff! Over here!" He waved his arms out the window and yelled "Over Here! We're over here!"

Mike reached up and grabbed the back of his shirt. Pulling him down, he quietly said "They know that by now, but if you keep shouting so will everything else!"

Leon looked at him and glared "They need help, let's go." He drew his sword and turned towards the door, only to be faced with a hulking husk filling the doorway, and blocking their path. Shrieking, the husk swung his arms, hitting Leon back against Mike, knocking them both down. As the creature leapt on top of the both of them. Leon slashed out with his blade, just catching the husk's neck. Blood sprayed all over them as the headless corpse landed on the two. The head sailed over them and hit the floor, rolling into a corner. Leon shoved the still bleeding corpse off of them and rolled to his feet, followed soon by Mike as he picked himself up. Retrieving his hammer from where it fell, Mike looked to Leon and growled. Leon nodded and said "Let's get moving."

Meanwhile, the fighting still raged in the streets as the hole closed behind them. Jeff looked at Jack and shouted "Well Alpha, any ideas or are we going to sit here balls deep in these shitheads all night?"

"I'm working on it, jackass just keep swinging." Jack spun his staff and cracked the head of a demon trying to get behind him. Thinking quickly, Jack sent a bolt of lightning through a nearby car, igniting the fuel tank into a fiery explosion. The force of the explosion sent a powerful shockwave through the surrounding horde, followed by a fiery wall. The attack sent the horde scattering and knocked many off their feet. As they scrambled to resume their attack, Jack and Jeff bolted off the mound and raced down the street. As they ran, Jack scanned the area around them trying to find a way out of the open and get back to the pack. Scanning the houses and buildings, he saw the shadow's moving through the buildings on his side. His nerves built as he noticed groups of demons breaking off, chasing after some unknown intruder.

Eventually, the two led the demons into a small children's park, where they killed off the remaining forces. Clear for a moment, Jeff doubled over, panting as he struggled to regain his breath. When he could breathe steady again, he said "Shit went to hell quickly huh?"

Jack laughed and he shook his head, too breathless to answer with words. As they drew their breath and looked around, Jeff said "Maybe we should get out of the open, we're sittin ducks out here." Just as Jack went to answer, a light flashed in one of the houses. The two looked at each other with uncertainty, then they crept toward the door, trying to move slowly to conserve their power.

Arriving at the door, Jack used the base of his staff to force the door open. As it swung open, they were greeted by Mike, who reached out and grabbed the two in each hand. Pulling them into the house, he embraced them both in a huge bear hug. Holding them both, he could barely contain his tears as he said "Jack, Jeff, you're back." He started to cry, and Jack pulled away to let Jeff and his brother fully embrace. He turned his attention to Leon and smiled "So she called in reinforcements huh? I guess." He smiled as Leon bowed and said "It's good to see you again bro."

Jack and Leon grasped forearms and embraced in a warrior's hug. When they pulled away, Leon placed his fist across his breast and bowed his head, and chuckled. When he met Jack's eyes, his mouth split open in a huge grin and he said through his laughter "We've missed you, alpha. I am surprised you've returned to us." Jack couldn't help but grin at Leon's face as he replied "The gods blessed us, my brother. Erebus literally broke the underworld to get us back here." Leon whistled his admiration, just as Jeff and Mike pulled away. Jeff rested his forehead against his brother's, whispering "I missed you bro."

Mike looked into his eyes and grasped his forearm, saying "And I you, my brother." Turning to Jack, he bowed his head "Don't think I've forgotten about you, my Alpha. I'm happy to have you back."

Jack returned the gesture, saying "Thanks big guy. I'm happy to be back."

"Alright" Leon looked out of the sitting room window, into the street. He saw husks stumbling and staggering, but moving closer to the house. He drew his blade and said "We need to move. We've got a base camp set up in the woods. We can party and celebrate your comeback when we've got that fucker's head on a pike."

"Agreed." Jeff cracked his knuckles and his neck, his eyes lighting up with the desire for vengeance "I want payback for that little trip to hell." Leon shook his head, smiling. "Hell only pissed you off, huh big guy?"

"Damn straight." Jeff hefted his axe over his head, and rested the head on his shoulder. Mike did the same with his hammer, and Jack rolled his shoulders. Seeing everyone make ready, Leon peered back out and observed the situation. Seeing the number of husks grow, and get closer, he said "If we're going to move, we need to do it now. The demons are scattered for now, but we've only got a few moments before they regain their senses." One by one, the group snuck through the door and made for the towns edge.

Back at camp Jasmine, James, and Serenity sat around the table, examining the local maps. Serenity took a small pocket knife and stabbed it through the location where the cabin was, marking it. The blade punctured the wood and left small splinters on the ground. Jasmine stood across from her, looking over notebook pages with lists of supplies for survival, lists of local flora that might be useful, and summaries of the terrain with the best and worst places to fight. She shook her head, saying "We've got to cross the majority of the town to get to this bastard. That means crossing this entire horde of demons." She looked at James, who was sitting on a small stump on his phone, scrolling through the local website. and asked "How many people were in this town before it turned?"

Without looking up, he responded "About three thousand, give or take a few dozen."

"Grand." Serenity's words were dry with sarcasm. Shaking her head, she tore her gaze to the map. In a huff, she pushed herself off the table and turned away, walking over to the cooler that they took from a neighboring site. Grabbing a coke, she popped the top and began to drink.

In the middle of her drink, Jasmine and James gasped and a familiar voice rang through the campsite "Honey, I'm home." Choking, she gasped, looked up, and saw Jack walking through the brush. She dropped the can on the ground, spilling the contents all over the dirt. She stood there, overcome with joy and wonder. Tears began to flood her eyes as she ran up and jumped into his arms, crying as he held her. As Jack sunk to the ground, cradling serenity in his arms, Jeff also emerged from the brush, followed by Mike and Leon, who proclaimed with joy "Look who we brought back."

James and Jasmine walked around Jack and Serenity, moving to hug Jeff. Jas's mouth fell open as she wrapped his arms around his neck. James was shaking his head in disbelief, but finally, he broke the silence by saying "How in the actual fuck did you two manage to get kicked out of DEATH?!" He threw his hands up and started to laugh as he continued "I mean, for real, what the actual hell did you guys do that got you banished?"

Serenity ignored the conversation and buried her face into Jack's shoulder, feeling the soft fabric of his shirt, and the solid muscles of his neck and shoulder. Her hair fell in front of her face, obscuring the tears that fell like rain drops form her eyes. Jack sat with her on the ground, rocking her gently and stroking her hair. She couldn't believe it, the man she loved was back. Her face trembled as she looked up slowly at him, convinced she had lost it. Slowly, she raised her hand and lightly touched his face and whispered "Jack." He nuzzled his face into her palm slightly and nodded. Seeing his blue eyes sparkle as they bobbed up and down, she let loose a torrent of tears.

Jeff looked at the two of them and said "Hey, where's my love?"

"I'll jump in your arms." James snickered as he jumped onto Jeff and tackled him, fake crying as he wailed "Oh Jeffy, It's so good to have you back."

The sight earned some soft laughs from the group, but they quickly silenced as Serenity quieted down. Wiping her eyes as she spoke, she said "I- I don't know what to say. I thought we lost you forever."

"Nah, Jack wouldn't let a tiny thing like death keep you from him." Jeff smiled as he patted Jack's back, continuing "Plus, I got tired of all the easy treatment I was getten anyway. Wanted to come back to the struggle of life." Serenity smiled up at the axe wielding blondie. Shaking her head, she rose up from Jack's lap. She strode over to Jeff and wrapped her arms around his neck in a friendly embrace. When she pulled away, she smiled at him and said "It's good to have you both back."

Jack looked around, examining their immediate area and remembered the walk back. He shook his head at the scenes of death and corruption and said "Well, shit's really going downhill fast here ain't it?"

You've got no idea." Jasmine responded flatly as she pointed to the map, which now had a small circle around it. "This tiny circle is where we stand, keeping nature alive. The area around it" she waved her hand a crossed the rest of the paper "has been corrupted by some kind of dark force. We can't get a reading on its power, so we've got no idea how strong it is."

James piped up "We can't get a solid foothold anymore. It's like a sickness spread across the land, slowly draining the life from it."

Jack looked back at the land around them. Outside their circle, the trees looked sickly and yellow, their leaves hanging by a thread. The grass was dry and crunchy, not a soft vibrate green that they expected. There was no birdsong, no rustling of squirrels or deer, even the wind seem stilled by the powers that be. Jack's heart went heavy at the sight of the dying land. He shook his head as he said "We need to end this thing, now."

He looked to his family, his pack. Years of work and skill passed as he forged them together and wrought a group that had defended against the darkest evil: Psychotic necromancers, demonic soldiers, and past ghosts have dogged them unending. Suddenly, all he could feel is pride. When he looked around, he saw the skill that defeated The Butcher and saved Troy. He saw the people that saved a young boy from demonic assaults, and the people who became a family when their biological parents failed. He took a moment to gather his thoughts, and spoke "I know, we've all been through a lot. We've fought necromancers, demonic spirits, creatures who would do wrong. We've freed minds and hearts from oppression, we lifted souls from possessions. We've shared in each other's grief and revealed in our joys. I've lead you through fiery hells and frozen darkness.

I'm honestly proud to fight by all of you, but I need to know something." Walking up to Serenity, he took her hand and turned back to the group "Will you fight with me again? Will you go with me one more time into the breach and slay this monster?"

Mike looked at his brother and snorted. He met Jack's eyes and smiled "Ya had to ask little one? Of course." Putting his hammer to the ground, his voice grew deep and somber as he said "My hammer stands ready to level the walls we will face."

Following his brother's lead, Jeff put the head of his axe in the dirt, saying "My axe stands ready to bathe in the blood of our enemies."

Jas walked up beside her lover and rested her hand on his shoulder. Her eyes sparkled with pride and power as she cracked her whip off her arm, saying "My whip will be the last thing they feel before the void claim's their tortured souls." She smiled at her mate and added "Besides, better ride and die with the pack, then live alone."

Leon drew his katana, flipped it around, and stuck it point first into the ground "I took an oath when I joined up: Stand strong in the face of evil, Speak the truth, even if it leads to your undoing. Safe guard the helpless and defend the land. I take that oath very seriously. On my honor, I'll help end this madness."

James's face twisted into a crazed smile, his knives unsheathed and crossed behind his head. "Well, since we're all being so serious, let me just say this." His smile faded and he said softly "To the end of time, I fight for this family."

Serenity looked at Jack and said "My arrows and spear will find the mark, and we will cleanse this horrible world." She kissed her fiance as he raised his staff in the air and said "Then tonight, my brothers, rest and relax. Tomorrow, we march."

A feeling of pride and strength flowed through the pack, pulsating through the air as they smiled and raised their own weapons to join his. Each knowing that tomorrow may be their last day on this realm.

Chapter Twelve: The Storm of War.

Rays of golden light streamed through the weak canopy. The golden beams fell onto Jack as he sat upon a small stump. A slight gleam of dew clung to his armor as he sat motionless, deep in meditation. As he felt the light and slight warmth hit his face, Jack opened his eyes. He had spent the night trying to focus his energy for the battle ahead.

As the sun continued its climbed rose through the tree tops, he rose from the stump where he sat. A faint smile crossed his lips, a familiar rush of energy as he prepared to face his enemies. Not for the first time since his escape from the underworld, he marveled at the craftsmanship of the gods. The armor was sturdy and strong, made of blackened leather and thick fibers. He held up his arms, marveling his new bracers. They sparkle slightly, as small specks of dew sparkled against the blacker-than-void leather. The inscribed runes thrummed softly as magic pulsed through them, giving Jack more power for his spells and protection for his hands. With practiced motion and skill, he rolled his shoulders and began stretching, testing the full range of motion he had. Satisfied, he picked up his staff from where it lay in the grass and stood, smiling into the sun.

When he turned to rouse the others, he noticed a large black chest had been placed in the fire pit overnight. The chest was made of dark wood, with bands of iron laid across it. On the top of the lid, sat a pentagram surrounded in laurels was carved into the wood. The hinges and handle were forged from polished bronze, and shown in the sun. When he approached it, he noticed a small note, hooked through the handle, fluttering in the soft breeze that blew through camp. Pulling it from the hook on the chest, he read it softly "Take these and give them to your pack, a symbol of our thanks for your loyalty."

Opening the box, he gasped in wonder. Packed within its depths were new sets of armor, each forged to the specific size of each member of the pack. Along with each armor set, the chest was further packed with matching combat boots and bracers for their forearms. The stacks were individually bound by silver silk rope, with each pack members name on small notes. The boot laces were tied together, with similar notes marking them. He lifted Serenity's set, marveling at how light it was. The women received a darkened, sleeveless, leather backed shirt and matching leggings. The men got similar shirts, but had heavy denim and leather patchwork cargo pants to wear. Each set had matching black combat boots, and black leather bracers for their forearms.

As he returned the armor to the trunk and finished his meditations, noise began to stir through the camp. Slowly, his pack mates began stirring from within the two tents that sat in the small campsite. As they shook the sleep from their bodies, Jack motioned toward the chest and said "The gods decided to bless us today guys. Take a look." Jeff, who was the first to wake up, shuffled over and opened the lid. His jaw dropped and all he could muster was "Ooohhh, those are beautiful." He pulled his set from the chest and quickly donned it. Flexing his arms and chest, he marveled at the range of motion and power he had. Looking around, he smiled and said "Well, looks like we got some serious gear. Let's kick some demon ass." He picked up his axe and swung it around, feeling the flow and motion of the armor and his weapon.

Jasmine and Mike emerged from the tent they shared with Serenity, and marveled at Jeff's new armor. Mike went over to the chest and pulled out his and Jasmine's suits. Tossing her set to Jasmine, Mike changed out of his dirty, disheveled clothes that he has been wearing since the fight first started. He started by slipping the heavy cargo pants up to his waste. Cinching the sewn in belt to secure the pants, he slipped the shirt over his broad shoulders and shook his head through the hole. He whistled softly and rotated his shoulders and swung his arms about. A small chuckle escaped his lips as he said "It's like Yule, or my birthday." After he felt the new clothes, he took his boots from the chest and slipped them on his feet. He laced them up, and slipped his new bracers on as he waited for the others.

Jas hooted and cheered "This is great! Now we have some decent fuckin gear." Donning her shirt, she flexed her arms, causing her Celtic knot work cross tattoo to expand "It even shows all my ink! This is great."

Serenity was next to emerge, drawn by all the hooting and hollering. "What's going on out here?" Rubbing the sleep from her eyes, she noticed the new armor that everyone was wearing. Her eyebrow raised as she asked "Where's my new gear, or did you guys forget about me?"

"Right here honey." Jack handed her the set that was labeled for her. As she wiggled into it, she asked "Where did this come from baby?"

"Erebus and the Lady Nyx. They helped Jeff and I escape hell and now I guess they're giving us some new armor."

Serenity whistled softly "I guess we need to be extra generous with our offerings when the next holiday rolls around." Jack nodded his agreement as he laced up his boots. She did the same thing as James and Leon woke up, and crawled out of their tent. Leon stared at the chest and the new armor, then he said "Fuckin A!" Bolting to the chest, he grabbed his armor and quickly put it on, sliding his katana through the back straps when he was finished. He flexed and admired how it looked as he said "Well shit, now I look like my role."

"What would that be dear brother?" James scoffed as he put on his own suit.

"Why, the dashing swordsman of course." He slicked his hair back and wiggled his eyebrows. James rolled his eyes as he put his on. His smile radiated his approval as he put his duel blades in their sheaths "Looks like this was made with us in mind, huh?" He looked at Jack and asked "I noticed you didn't bed down last night. What's the plan big dog?"

Jack looked at his pack. Each one dressed in a sleek, black set of battle armor. A feeling of pride swelled within his breast as Jack inspected them. Before he responded, closed the lid of the chest and replaced the table over the pit. When it was back in place, Jack motioned for them to join him at the planning table. When they were all gathered around, he started "Ok, we've got a lot of ground to cover in a single push. What I was going to say was that we fan out, engulfing the town in power so we weaken the horde, and once we purify the town, we move in and surround the demon."

"A loose plan, it leaves a lot of room for error." Jasmine raised her eyebrow and continued "Are you sure about this Jack? No time table or anything?"

Jack shook his head "We don't have time or a need for it Jas. This is a straightforward engagement. We move in, wipe the floor with the demon and his horde, fix the land and move out."

Mike and Jeff looked at each other. Jeff grunted, already entering a vicious mindset, then Mike said "Jeff and I will move right through the center, making as much noise as we can. We'll draw the majority of them to us and slaughter them."

Leon looked at them and said "I'm going with you."

Serenity looked at them and said "I'll get on a roof top and shadow you guys from above. With some luck, I can drop some with my bow and thin them out."

Jasmine sighed, putting her head in her hands. A feeling of uncertainty washed over her. She hated when there wasn't a true plan on the table. Sighing, she squared her shoulders and said "Jack and I are the two most powerful of the pack, so we will make a beeline for the demon's nest and kill it quickly."

James looked around and groaned "Looks like I'm running solo." He flipped his duel swords around and smiled "I'll run interference. Keeping them from coming at the side or up at Serenity."

Jack took one last look around. He saw his pack standing as ready as they could be, with the plan in mind. Satisfied with them, then he looked to the sky. The sun was cresting over the trees, casting their long dark shadows on the ground below. He looked back to his pack and said "We don't have a lot of time before this land dies and takes these people with it. Let's go kick some demon ass. We make for the town limits and once we get to it, we split up and keep our roles. Remember your oaths." With that, he retrieved his staff from where it leaned against a tree, and led his pack out into the woods.

The pack fanned out between the trees, moving slowly. There was no words exchanged between the group, only glances and nods, keeping everyone moving in sync through the forest. Jack stood at the lead, making sure everyone could keep a visual on him as he blazed the trail. All around him, the group moved like ghost, soft and soundless. Each person was filled with apprehension and adrenaline as they moved closer to the town.

Suddenly, Jack raised his fist, signaling the stop. Between them and the edge of the forest, sat a large camp, complete with an RV and several tents. Milling between the structures, were at least a dozen husks. Jack crouched behind a fallen log, and seeing that, the rest of the group took cover as well. Jack surveyed the situation, weighing their options. After a few moments of debate, he let a soft growl rumble, signaling his decision to fight. Upon hearing it, the rest of the group shuffled, readying their weapons. Jack waited a few more moments, watching as the husks aimlessly wandered through. He waited for one to get close enough to him, and when it finally happened, he launched himself out from the tree line. The husk was knocked to the ground by the force of the hit, and Jack brought his fist down on the creature's neck. A sickening snap, followed by a worse gurgle was heard as Jack stood and smiled. The rest of the husks rushed at him, only to be met with the rest of the group, charging from cover and meeting them with steel. A short skirmish ensued as the group cleared the husks.

In short order, the husks were dead. Jack looked around and checked the group for any serious injuries. Finding nothing but a few scratches, he signaled them forward. When they reached the town limits, Jack motioned for them to form the circle. They sat upon the ground and hummed softly while Jack spoke "Wolves of war, hunters of demons and slayers of monsters, we call you now. Help us heal this land, once green and lush. A terrible evil has fell over it, making it sickly and dead. Bind with us, oh immortal hunters of old, so that we may rid this land of darkness."

The pack turned their gaze to the sky as black storm clouds rolled into the sky. Then, the binding happened. One by one, the pack began to change and morph. Jack and Mike sprouted black fur, their eyes changed to a bloody, crimson red. They grew in height until they each stood about seven foot tall apiece. They rose up on two legs, standing tall as their armor returned to their bodies. Mike gripped his hammer's haft as he planted the head in the dirt. Jack did the same with his staff, but he rolled his shoulder as a wicked looking great sword took its place across his back. The two shook the water from their fur and watched as the rest changed.

Jeff also had black fur, but his wolf was different. The body was covered in crimson markings, and two horns sprouted from his head. His eyes sparkled a deep, blood red as he too, rose and joined Jack and Mike. He looked to Jack, and bowed his head, a gravely "Alpha." Escaping his lips. He hefted his axe, which had also transformed into a powerful looking weapon. Two heads, wrought of blackened steel sat on an iron haft, which came to a deadly point on the bottom. With force, he planted the axe and waited.

Serenity's fur came in a soft, glowing red. Her body didn't budge with muscle, like the males, but rather became a wiry, tight frame. In her hand, came a recurved bow, made from dark oak. She stood, and a quiver full of black and silver arrows lay across her back. In her free, outstretched hand, a silver spear with an obsidian head rose from the ground and into her hand. Her eyes changed into a deep, rich amber. She grew as well, but not as tall as the men, standing just under six and a half feet.

Jasmine's fur grew into a deep, smoky grey, with eyes to match. She rose and reached her hand to the sky. In that instant, a brilliant flash of light broke the darkness, and carried a golden bullwhip into her waiting grasp. Taking the handle, she smiled a vicious smile as she unfurled it and struck the sky, causing it to cackle and hum as lightening pulsed through it.

James sprouted fur that took a deep, rich brown, with eyes of sparkling silver. He grew to a height of six feet. Two twisted daggers of bronze hung in an X across his back. The leather wrapped handles stuck out on either side of his neck, and the pommels formed solid spheres of bronze.

Leon, being the newest, changed last. His fur was a mixture of black and white, with eyes that shown like polished onyx. His armor was the only one to change, as it became styled after the samurai of old. His katana, once wore across his back, now saw on his hip in a black painted sheath. He pulled a soft, cloth face mask from the inside of the chest piece and settled it across his nose, so that only his eyes shown.

When they had all settled, Jack drew the wicked looking sword and placed his staff through the loops. As he drew them tight, he growled "Let's move." One by one, they split up. Jasmine and Jack split off and skirted the town wide, heading for the beach. James feel back into the shadows and drew his blades, ready to follow Serenity to her perch. Jeff, Leon, Mike, and Serenity looked at each other, and threw back their heads in a vicious war howl. All the while, the rains fell.

Jack and Jasmine ran ahead, in a wide arc of the town. When they reached the beach, however, their progress was slowed by the number of husks that filled the sand. They slowed to a complete stop, and watched as the husks descended upon them. Jack raised his blade and let the rain catch on it. It was a double edged sword, with a narrow bill on the central point, just below the point. A single fuller grove ran down the center, separating the straight edge, from the serrated edge. Jasmine unfurled her whip and began twirling it above her head, causing clouds to swirl behind them and lightening to pulse through. Jack heard the war howl of the others, and his own blood hammered through his veins. A twisted smile ran across his lips as he waited for the husks to group together and gain ground to them. When they were within distance, he lashed out in a vicious arc, and Jasmine unleashed the lighting.

All the while, the other group charged into town. They howled, growled and challenged the demons around them. The sound of their challenges echoed between the buildings, and shook the windows in their frames. Soon, they had a horde of them chasing them, and more crawling, scrambling and climbing out of the houses in a vain attempt at surrounding them. Serenity leaped up to a nearby roof top and unleashed a storm of arrows into the throng of demons that perused the pack. Each of her silver and black arrows finding their mark in a demon's chest or head, some with enough force to knock them to the ground, causing some of the husks to trip and stumble over the bodies of their fallen.

James jumped up next to her and spun his blades around in a twirling dance of death. His bronze blades danced and struck like bolts of lighting, carving a nearby demon to pieces. When he could, he used the pommels of his daggers to smack the husks from the rood. Serenity looked to him just as he did one such move, a sickening crunch came from a head as he caved in a husk's skull, then booted him from the roof. Seeing her looking to him, James gave a sheepish yet twisted grin and shrugged his shoulders. Serenity said nothing to him, but returned the smile and nodded to James. Jumping from rooftop to rooftop, Serenity and James shadowed Jeff, Mikey, and Leon from above, firing arrows and keeping them clear.

As they ran, Mike and Jeff were knocking demons aside and sending them flying through the air, crashing into houses, cars, light posts, and through windows. While they were running and keeping a path clear, Leon kept stride in between them, constantly looking for a place open enough to make a stand. As more husks joined the fray, the trio slowed, and Leon was forced to draw his blade. As he drew, he hit a husk in the stomach with the pommel of his katana, then brought the blade through his neck as he drew, taking the head clean off. As the blood sprayed in his face, he finally found the open town square. He pointed toward the main downtown square and ran ahead of the brothers. Following him, Mike and Jeff ran into the square and stood back to back with Le, forming a triangle. Serenity jumped on the roof of a two story business almost directly above them and resumed her firing. She pointed below her and growled "James, Get down below and keep them from reaching me up here. I don't care how you do it, but keep my ass clear."

He growled back "With pleasure, my queen." With that, he jumped into an attic and stood at the stairwell. Soon, he heard the shattering of glass, followed by the thud of boots and shoes running up the stairs. The sharp, nonsensical screeching noises of the husks came ahead of them as they rounded the landing and started up to the second floor. Jester grinned, settled into a crouch, and snarled "Let's play." Growling and screaming with rage, the demons rushed him. Three fit up the stairs at a time, making it difficult for the rest to move. Jester smiled with glee as he jumped sideways, planting his foot to the wall. He spun over their heads and cut them off as he flew.

He landed at the bottom of the stairs and looked around. He stood in the attic, his blood covered face formed a twisted smile as more demons charged up the stairs. He spun his bronze blades around and engaged them, blood spurting from stumps of heads and limbs. He caught his last opponent's arm in an X-block, grinning, he spun out and kicked the husk's legs out. As it fell to its knees, Jester's teeth flashed in a wicked grin as he twirled his blades around and laid them in an X shape across its shoulders. In one swift motion, he crossed them, decapitating his last foe for a time. Looking back toward the roof, he shouted "How are you doing, Serenity?"

She growled back "Fine, just trying to keep them down for the boys. Keep up the good work."

He turned back and saw another wave enter his floor Grinning he said softly to himself "I love my job." Howling, he dove into the small throng of demons, his blades disappearing in a wave of slashing and hacking, carving the demons into pieces.

While James defended Serenity's perch on the roof, Jeff, Mike, and Leon stood in the square. Once a thriving park area, the land was now dead. The trees hung leafless and dry, the grass crunched under their feet, and the once bright and colorful children's play ground was now covered with bodies and blood. Jeff drove the head of his axe into the chest of a demon foolish enough to rush into his path. As it doubled over, stunned, he quickly turned to Mikey "How are you holding up brother?" He swung his axe up and caught the husk under the chin, splitting the head. As the body fell, he turned to face the next group that charged him.

Mikey turned and growled "Watch as they go flying." His deep voice boomed with twisted laughter as he knocked them back with his hammer, sending two flying at a time. He watched with pleasure as they sailed in the air before crashing into a metal jungle gym. The bodies crumpled over the bars and sat there motionless. Turning to Leon, he asked "How do you fare, young one?"

Leon snarled as he pulled his katana from the chest of a demon and cut its head off in a furious slash. Growling in response, he said "I'm fine, just let me work." He dodged an attack and followed with a series of slashes that diced his opponent to pieces. As the body fell apart into a bloody mess, he jumped through a swing set and impaled a husk coming up on Jeff's flank. Under his breath, Leon mumbled "Jack and Jas better hurry, or we may be over run." He growled as he charged his next set of opponents.

Meanwhile, Jack and Jasmine ran through the forest in full wolf form. As they emerged from the tree line, they returned to their symbote form and stood motionless. Jack's eyes darted back and forth, checking the clearing and the cabin for any signs of movement. His grip on the blade tightened and loosened repeatedly as he detected nothing. Keeping his eyes on the cabin, he growled to Jasmine "Fan out, we'll take the house from both sides."

Snarling, she grunted and simply said "Right." Fanning out, they surrounded the house and stepped into the clearing. The rain shown on the grass and trees, bringing the land slowly back to life.

As they approached, the demon's hissing laughter rang out from the cabin. Slowly, the creature sauntered out and wheezed "Again, three ancients meet upon fields of red, one to be left for dead. Would that a twisted soul have a last stand, the blood of innocence in demand. Daresay you will let me speak my plea, or do you intend to silence me?"

Jack snarled "No more rhymes or tricks, you nameless coward. Speak your intent and let us end this fight." He took his stance and leveled the blade in front of his body while Jas unfurled her whip.

The demon's twisted smile spread across his pale face and he said "A trade in my mind, one that will leave me behind. Your pack will turn your back and let me be, Is that a deal to offer me?"

Jas growled and snarled "You slaughter and destroy innocent people, turning them into monsters. You mock and attack us and kill two of our own, and you have the balls to ask for mercy?" She cracked the whip against the ground. The furrow it left bore deep into the earth, allowing the rain water to pool in the dirt. Just as the whip took the energy from the lighting of the sky, it changed into a flexible, yet strong willow whip.

Jack raised an eyebrow, but said nothing as his attention returned to the demon "Speak, you insolent wyrm. We will offer you a chance to share what you claim to know before we send you back to whatever foul cesspit you crawled from."

The demon's wheezing laughter came forth louder, as he replied "A darkness, a shroud shall cover the land, from mountain to sea none will stand. An evil so powerful, the world will rock. Demons from all ways, all walks. A great war tearing the world to sunder, a darkness that will pull all under."

It was Jack's turn to snarl as he shot back "NEVER! We are the guardians of this world, and we have seen nothing of what you speak. I've had enough of your lies and tricks. I'm going to end your miserable, wretched life." With that, Jack rushed the demon with his sword raised. He swung at an arc, trying to catch the freak's neck. But the demon was too swift, and dove to the side. In a swift, almost practiced motion, Freak caught Jack's wrist and delivered a series of stunning blows to his stomach and face, causing Jack to stumble and drop his blade. Jas lashed out at the creature with her whip, trying to bind him. As the blow came, the Freak side stepped it and rushed her. Before Jack could interfere, the Freak caught Jas by the throat and lifted her high. Another round of wheezing laughter came from his mouth "I've lived for thousands of years or more, I've sent many to death's dark door. You will stand no threat to me, The Freak of Eternity."

The demon tossed Jas to the ground, and clustered energy around his fist to smash into her face. The Freak laughed and prepared to strike a fatal blow, until Jack jumped in the way and caught his fist. Jack then hit Freak with a powerful uppercut, sending the demon sailing through the air, back toward the cabin. He took a stance over Jas, to buy her time to get back to her feet. When she was back to her feet, they circled the Freak. Snarling and snapping, but saying no words. As the demon rose to his feet, Jack rushed over and delivered a powerful kick that sent Freak sprawling in the dirt.

Jack smiled as he felt the ribs crack from his kick. He turned to Jas and motioned toward the house with his head "Go see what you can dig up, I'll finish up here." As she moved toward the door, Jack walked to where his blade had fell from his grasp. Picking it up, he strode back to where the Freak was on his hands and knees. His laughter came out more wheezing and strained than usual, a small pool of black blood pooling in his hand that he held over his chest.

"Power of the gods light of divine, such power is the match of mine. A great warrior clashes with the harbinger of chaos. Would that I wield such powerful might, which would cause such a fright." His laughter got strained as Jack snarled back "In the end, the hunters rule the day. You could never stand up to the guardians of the world." He stood over the Freak, who was now struggling to stand. Jack held his blade as he delivered another kick, knocking the demon over onto his back.

Jack placed his foot on the Freaks chest, feeling the ribs crack and break under his boot. He planted the head of his blade in the dirt on the opposite side of the Freaks neck, making it a chopping block. Jas went around into the cabin to find the energy pool. Outside, she heard the sickening *schlick* as Jack cut the Freaks head off, and the subsequent thump of the head being kicked against the wall. While she waited for him to join her, she looked around the interior of the cabin. It was vampyric in design and interior, complete with arched doorways and columns etched into the walls beside any threshold. The stone and wood were etched with symbols of Nyx and Erebus, along with a few other, minor lords. Above the fireplace, the remnants of a tattered flag could still be seen. On top of it all, there was obvious signs of the demon's extended living within its walls. The floors were scorched black with burn marks and the walls had splatters of dried blood, and furrows of claw marks. Furniture was over turned and blackened by repeated blasts of that dark energy. She knelt down and touched the wooden floors, imagining what it would've looked like when the coven lived here. As she shook her head, Jack stepped through the doorway, sword in sheath, staff in hand. Jas looked around and said "We need to find this energy pool and fast, otherwise we'll never release those people from their hell."

Jack stepped further inside and looked around. Pointing to the back corner, he said "Look." Jas looked over and saw a small doorway with a stairwell that was leading down. Jack summoned a ball of pure white light and had it hover above his staff. Looking and Jas, he led the way down the stairs and into the cellar.

Back at the town, the warriors were getting hard pressed to hold their ground. Leon was being backed down a small alleyway, unable to get around the sheer mass of bodies that pressed in on him. Sweat poured down his brow, stinging his eyes. His blade began to feel heavy, and his breathing became labored. Unable to resist anymore, he called out "Any time you guys could get your asses over here and bail me out, that would be lovely." He kicked a husk over a small mound of corpses, buying some time.

"I've got my own problems." Mike was being pressed away from the rest by the shear mass of bodies that piled in between them. His hammer grew heavy as he swung it down on another head. He hollered over to Jeff "Bro, can you give him a hand?"

Jeff snarled back "Hell no!" He threw a smaller axe into the chest of a nearby demon that was flanking him, then he crashed the head of his axe into the chest of another. "I'm a little busy at the moment." He looked up to Serenity's roof top in fear.

Up top, she was clashing with two demons at once that had climbed up the back wall and surpassed Jester's blockade. They we all cut off, surrounded, and running out of options. Serenity yelled down "Get up here if you can. It's better that we all die as one."

Hearing her call, Leon immediately disengaged his opponents with a swift kick to the chest. As they stumbled over the bodies, he climbed on top of a dumpster, grabbed a window ledge, and proceeded to climb up onto the roof. When he was within reach, he jumped to the ledge and pulled himself up and onto the roof. He found himself placed close to Serenity, and rushed over, blade drawn to assist. He drew his breath and said "It's good to see you in one piece. When the arrow's stopped falling, I thought something happened to you." He impaled a husk as he went.

Serenity huffed and responded "I got attacked from behind." She motioned with her head to the five other corpses around her. "They got smart and climbed up the wall instead of trying to go through the clown down there." A wheezing bout of cackling laughter rose as James screamed "DIE YOU STUPID FUCKER!"

On the street level, Jeff and Mike managed to fight themselves back together. Jeff was breathing heavy and looked to his brother "I don't think I'll get another chance if I go down again bro. I just wanna say" he was interrupted momentarily as he dodged a swipe from a crawling husk. He brought his axe down on his head as he said "I love you big guy, and thanks for having my back all these years." Mike looked back at his brother, and with a weary sigh, he said "We're family, always have been, always will be. I love you too lil bro." With that, the brothers turned together and howled as one, diving into the demon force with power and strength, driving them back as fast and as hard as they could.

Chapter Thirteen: Endgame.

Jack and Jas walked down into the cellar. Racks that once held jars of food or bottles of wine and other drinks were shattered. Skeletons littered the floor, some still had bits of old, rotten flesh still clinging to the bare bones. Their wolf eyes allowed for good sight in the dimly lit space. Unfortunately, there sense of smell could pick up every little thing. The scent of rotting, putrid flesh. The stench of mold and mildew and dust filling the air. The worst was the silence. Even their footsteps seemed to fall with complete silence, despite their heavy combat boots.

Jas scanned the room, then looked to Jack "Wow. The Freak really did a number on this place." Jack said nothing, his gaze sweeping the old, decrepit room. That's when he saw it. His gaze found a doorway, concealed by an old shelving unit. With a swift motion of his hand, Jack cast the rickety old shelf to the ground. The wood splintered and broke as it hit the stone floor. As he did, Jack studied the doorway. Roughly six feet high and four feet wide, it resembled an older style door. Colum's etched in the stone and a rounded top gave away the vampyric design. He steeled himself and touched the stone; feeling the hard, cold marble under his fingers. The stone hummed faintly as the last remnants of magic still clung to the shattered doorway.

Jas peered around the doorway, into the impossibly dark room, and said "I wonder if this the door that demon crawled from?" She looked around the door and that's when she noticed it: A small hole in the middle of the top. On a hunch, she summoned forth the gem and held it up. The ruby began to glow a soft red color. Jack noticed and regarded the inner area with new interest. Jas whistled softly and said "I wonder: Was this a lock, or something more?"

"Probably a lock, but then again, how could that demon: kill the vamps that lived here, poison the land, and make a weapon like that can completely reap and entire populous and possess them in such a short time." Jack replied as he cast his light inside. The room was empty. No bed, no slab, no nothing. The stones were blacked by repeated blasts of energy and multiple claw marks scarred the area around the door. The only thing that was in the room at all was a small, black iron box. It was maybe the size of a shoebox, but had a wrought iron look. The lid was carved with strange, unfamiliar runes that seemed to give off an unfamiliar energy.

Jack nodded toward Jas, who walked into the room and stomped on the lock with her boot. As she worked to break it open, Jack sat on the basement floor, just outside the room. He closed his eyes and began to chant. Soon, white tendrils sprouted from his dark fur and touched everything. The walls, ceiling and floor were all covered in white strands of healing energy.

The box lasted three stomps under Jas's boot before breaking. Once it was opened, a blinding blue light shot out and a whirlwind kicked up. The souls of the townspeople all escaped at once. As the energy swirled around, they could hear the souls within screaming and crying with happiness at their freedom. As they flew past Jack, he felt his spell bolster in strength as their joy and happiness radiated through the house, and into him. He had tears in his eyes as he finished his incantation and rose, smiling at Jas. Sprinting up the stairs, they ran outside to see the spirits fly into the sky above. The cooling rain fell to the ground as the energy of the townspeople healed the land.

Back in the town, things were looking grim. James had to pull back off the stairs, Serneity and Leon were being backed into corners, and Atlas and Goliath were swamped by a sea of husks. Then, just as the pack began to falter, a blue light streamed from the clouds, and flashed like lightening. Through the town, the souls of the townspeople flew, trying to find their bodies. Those who were still had bodies to reclaim, did so, causing that husk to collapse. Those who had lost their bodies in the fight, flew into the sky to join their heaven. Bit by bit, the army of husks collapsed as their souls returned. While the earth pulled the remains of the demons that were killed down into the soil. A tired howl of victory went up from the pack, as their wolves also receded and they turned human once more.

Epilogue

Jack and the pack looked back at the small town of Crystal Cove. Standing at a hill on the drive out of town. A bright, well-earned smile shown on every face as the survivors went about their daily lives. The sound of cars rumbled through the air, dogs barked, and the people were bustling through the town. Birds had returned to the trees, animals roamed the grass and forest again, and the fish had returned to the cove. Jack spoke the words aloud "The land is recovering. That's what we like to see." Leon stooped down and brushed his hand over the soft, green grass that was growing over the brittle, dried remains of the old. After the battle, another group of vampyres, posing as therapists, doctors, and shop keepers had moved back into the cabin to finish cleansing it and help the townspeople with their mental damage, physical trauma, and to restore commerce.

Jack pulled Serenity closer to him, sighing and kissing her forehead. Mike wrapped Jasmine in his arms, Jeff, James, and Leon stood with their arms over each other's shoulders. Jack looked around and said "Well guys, our work is done. I think that's the last we'll be seeing of that level of fuckery for a long time." With that said, the group turned and piled into Jack's truck and James's van.

Meanwhile in an isolated, underground cavern, a tall and lanky looking man stood. Surrounding him, carved into the walls, were runes in the same strange language. A soft dripping was heard from somewhere in the dark recesses of the cave. He was dressed in a fine black suit with a blood red tie. Hands clasped behind his back, he twisted and tapped the metal of a ring on his right hand. He stood, studying the runes that scrolled across the wall. From somewhere behind him, a door opened and closed again, and a twisted figure lurched up and bowed, saying "Master, the

Freak is dead and banished. We've lost the western gateway."

A smooth, velvety voice replied "The Freak was no big loss, he was just a means to an end." Holding up a blood red crystal, he said "We've got what we need. Soon the whole world will see things," he chuckled, "through a new eye." His booming laugh echoed through the cave as the red light danced off the strange crystal.